"I think I ~~...~~ beneficial barter," Bri said.

"Were you aware I worked in day care before moving here?"

Several expressions crossed Ian's face, including profound relief and gratitude. It grew as his gaze swept across the hall to hover protectively over the tiny sleeping beauty he loved with his whole heart.

That moment Bri knew some things for certain.

First, Ian Shupe was about to take her up on her offer to watch his daughter. Second, he could not be more handsome. And third, she'd have to keep her attraction at bay. It sprang out of nowhere as he turned from Tia to Bri and smiled like the sunrise.

Looking at him now, she knew her heart wasn't safe.

"Bri Landis, you're a lifesaver." He shook her hand. Then held it.

"And Ian Shupe, you're a godsend."

His face tightened. "I wouldn't say that."

"That's okay, because God would. And that's all I need to know for now."

Books by Cheryl Wyatt

Love Inspired

CHERYL WYATT

An R.N. turned stay-at-home mom and wife, Cheryl delights in the stolen moments God gives her to write action- and faith-driven romance. She stays active in her church and in her laundry room. She's convinced that having been born on a naval base on Valentine's Day, she was destined to write military romance. A native of San Diego, California, Cheryl currently resides in beautiful, rustic southern Illinois, but she has also enjoyed living in New Mexico and Oklahoma. Cheryl loves hearing from readers. You are invited to contact her at Cheryl@CherylWyatt.com or P.O. Box 2955, Carbondale, IL 62902-2955. Visit her on the web at www.CherylWyatt.com and sign up for her newsletter if you'd like updates on new releases, events and other fun stuff. Hang out with her in the blogosphere at www.Scrollsquirrel.blogspot.com or on the message boards at www.LoveInspiredBooks.com.

Doctor to the Rescue
Cheryl Wyatt

Love Inspired

 ™ LOVE INSPIRED BOOKS

ISBN-13: 978-0-373-81669-9

DOCTOR TO THE RESCUE

Then the Lord God formed a man from the dust of the ground and breathed into his nostrils the breath of life, and the man became a living being.
—*Genesis* 2:7

Mom and Dad: Your encouragement convinced me I could attain any dream I wanted. I took to heart every word of affirmation and praise you spoke. Every reader touched by these books is a result of the two of you championing my dreams and putting flight to every hope you gave me courage to have.

To my former OB crew at Memorial Hospital of Carbondale: I'm thankful for the opportunity to have worked with you as a nurse. Each of you left an indelible impression on my heart. Writing this medical miniseries brought back so many fond memories of you. Miss and love you all!

Lord: Thank You for unshackling my imagination and allowing me to write for You.

To Missy Tippens and Camy Tang: Thank you so much for your help brainstorming this series.

Lisa: You're the best sister in the world, and I am so thankful we are friends as well as family.

Melissa Endlich and Rachel Burkot: Thank you so much for your encouragement, editorial insight and expertise. I am blessed to be able to work with you!

Chapter One

Bri Landis's pulse lurched like the ladder beneath her feet.

With her waist at roof level, she clawed at the eaves of her run-down lake lodge, understanding her brother Caleb's caution to never climb alone. Heart thumping, Bri clutched the gutter. Ominous buckling. *No!*

It ripped free in a spray of rust and screeching metal. Screams tore through her as she plummeted...into a bush.

Bri could only gulp. Blink. Moan. She should have listened to her brother, she thought. Caleb was overseas on army medic duty instead of here at home in Eagle Point, Illinois, witnessing Bri make friends with her favorite shrub.

Now the shrub was squished and she was sprawled in it, lamenting her long hair. She disentangled her blond hair, then struggled to get upright amid a sharp sea of scarlet. Sweat beaded her forehead despite late-December's chill.

Her untimely ladder escapade put a painfully ironic twist on this being the last day of "fall."

Bri emerged, corky twigs crackling and biting like spindly wooden teeth. Jagged underbrush snagged her brother's favorite hoodie. Bri pulled it from the branches holding it hostage. *Gasp.*

Pain seared her left arm. She slid the cuff and looked at it. Unnatural angle. Disbelief slid through her like the ladder off the roof. No question: arm broken.

And with it all hope of meeting the bank's deadlines.

Dismay ran through her. Saving Landis Lodge—Eagle Point's only retreat center and her family heritage—from foreclosure, meant renovating and renting seven cabins by mid-February. Roughly one cabin a week. She'd sold the daycare she owned in Chicago and moved home to make it happen.

Now days from Christmas, she risked losing the last thing her late mother loved—the lodge Bri had inherited and promised to save. No way could she afford contractors.

Her teeth chattered. "Where's my stupid phone?" She needed help ASAP.

Forget going back into the bush to find her phone. A new trauma center sat right next door.

Bri held her arm high and stationary and bolted from her yard, not caring if she resembled a maniac.

Eagle Point Trauma Center came into view over a leafy hill.

She'd never been so glad to see a modern facility nestled against rustic Eagle Point Lake, stately risen bluffs, scenic trails and seriously fun caves. The serene landscape of Bri's childhood home calmed her against the mind-bending pain gnawing her arm.

Halfway to EPTC, dizziness hit Bri. She fell to her knees and clung to a parking barricade.

"She's hurt!" someone yelled across the lot. Bri couldn't be sure who it was. Nausea sent her face between her knees. Rapid footsteps pounding nearby pavement competed with the pulse *swoosh*ing her ears.

Strong hands gently braced her shoulders. "Hey, you okay?"

Her bad day just got worse.

Bri blinked up into the stunning aqua eyes of the absolute last person she wanted seeing her in this state.

Dr. Ian Shupe.

Yet, for the first time since meeting him weeks ago, concern and compassion emanated from the tall, dark and imposing anesthesiologist's normally sullen eyes. "What happened, Bri?"

"Ladder slid. I f-fell," she puffed past savage pain.

Ian's assessing eyes quickly roved over her. "How far?"

Tremors overtook her. "Maybe nine feet."

Did his face just pale? For sure, his jaw tightened. Probably thought she was an idiot. Ian's warm fingers felt soft yet strong and capable as they examined her elbow.

Kate, the center's surgical nurse, skidded in, dropped to her knees, took one look at Bri's injured arm and gave Ian a pointed look.

He nodded once. "Already saw it. Get a gurney and splints."

"Will do." Kate flashed Bri a strength-infusing smile, then dashed back toward the trauma center.

"C-collar, too," Ian called to Kate, then faced Bri again. Broad shoulders and impressive arms obviously well acquainted with a gym flexed and bunched as he maneuvered closer, training his eyes on her. His firm strength and sure demeanor erased her fears and convinced her that despite his terse reputation she was in good hands. "Where do you hurt most?"

"My left forearm. But I think I can walk the rest of—"

"No. In fact, don't move." Ian shirked off his suit coat, its raven color identical to his black military-style hair. Coat spread on asphalt, he settled Bri on it. His palms became her pillow. His gesture soothed. "Did you land on concrete?"

She started to shake her head but stopped when Ian's thumbs pressed against her temples, keeping her neck still.

"No. I landed in the waiting arms of a winged euonymus."

"A what?" Confusion amped up his cuteness.

"Big red hedge. More widely known as a burning bush."

A congenial nod seemed out of character for his usual surly self. His fingers kneaded and prodded her bones and muscles. Fierce concentration knit his brows. Had he any idea how handsome he was in doctor mode? Her arm might be broken, but nothing was wrong with her eyes. Bri chided herself for noticing the good doctor's bad-boy looks.

Not only had military deployments and divorce left him notoriously difficult and brooding, Bri's heart still felt raw after the end of a bad relationship with a verbally abusive boyfriend.

Her move from the Chicago suburbs to downstate Illinois had finally given her the long-needed courage to break up with Eric two months ago. If only he'd *stop* calling and harassing her. Dr. Shupe's abrasive manner reminded her too much of Eric. Except, Ian wasn't being curt and caustic now, but gentle and thorough.

Bri huffed at the physical exam. "Nothing's numb. Or tingly. Or blurry. I didn't hit my head or black out, either."

Ian's mouth twitched. Wrestling back a smile? She'd love to see it. She didn't think him capable of glee before now.

Bri sighed. "Sorry. Caleb's injury training wears off on me. I'm his study buddy and procedural guinea pig. He splints, tags, bandages, braces and bores the living daylights out of me for his military medic certifications and field practice exams."

The humor whispering along Ian's lips in a near smile spread to his eyes now, deepening them to a breathtaking blue. They turned serious and probing. "What were you doing on the ladder?"

"Renovating the lodge. Replacing eaves." *Or attempting to.*

"By yourself?"

Here came the lecture. She got enough of those from Caleb over her fierce determination to save Landis Lodge.

If she lost the lodge, she might also lose the memories, especially of childhood with Mom. Grief knotted her throat.

"Who else do I have?" She bit her lip as Ian's

eyebrows rose. But she had valid reasons to grouch. Her ex was a dud, her dad a deadbeat, her mom was deceased, her brother was deployed and a bank breathed ultimatums down her back. Now a broken arm ordeal that she didn't have time for. But it could have been much worse. *Lord, thank you for cushioning my fall.*

"Who's on call?" Bri instantly regretted her words. "You're obviously off duty and not who'd take care of me, since you're an *anesthest*—however you say it. I won't need one of those, right?"

Ian's vague expression did not make her feel good.

Lord, please don't let me need surgery. Ian's inexplicable rudeness since she'd moved back here proved she wouldn't be his first choice in a patient.

Her new friends, Lauren and Kate, had told her that Ian only acted abrasive because he was attracted to Bri in the wake of his unwanted divorce. Gibberish.

On the other hand, the girls had to be in the know, since they were nurses on Ian's trauma team. Plus Lauren's fiancé, Mitch, was Ian's best friend and lead trauma surgeon on the team. Ian suddenly flashed a penlight at her eyes, dotted with… "Fairy stickers?"

He smiled wryly. "My little daughter put them there." The five-year-old he'd been embroiled in

custody battles over. Ian would probably freak if
he knew how Bri knew about that. She focused
on the fairies to distract from excruciating arm
pain.

Kate arrived with a gurney and supplies. After
applying the neck brace, she brandished a pair of
bandage scissors.

"Don't cut my hoodie! It's Caleb's keepsake.
Please, I have a tank top underneath." The world
went sideways as they rolled Bri onto a backboard before righting her. Kate texted someone.

"I'll try. No guarantees." Ian eased the hoodie
off and splinted her arm as if he'd done it a hundred thousand times. Probably had, overseas during combat surgeries.

"Didn't realize you could do all that being an
anest—that."

Ian's mouth thinned into another smirk.

Kate leaned toward his ear. "Since your final
custody hearing's in an hour, I paged the nurse-
anesthetist on call."

Ian glanced at his watch. Scratched his jaw.
Addressed Kate in low tones. Bri heard mention of her brother's name. Caleb had commis-
sioned Ian to watch over her when he deployed
last week. Why Ian? Especially in light of Ian's
hostility toward her.

Then Caleb had suddenly dubbed Ian her bodyguard? What was up with *that?* She didn't need to be protected. Or babysat.

Ian plucked sage twigs, fiery leaves and feathers from her hair. "Nest?"

"Almost." Kate winked and strode in her usual militant but graceful fashion. How Kate could be runway-model pretty and a black belt was beyond Bri, but Kate was someone Bri was glad to know. Except she aimed a needle at her now.

Bri squished her eyes until the worst was over. Eyes open, she realized she'd not only grabbed Ian's arm but left crescent marks. Bri recoiled, fearing an acrid verbal assault like ones Eric was prone to.

But Ian didn't seem fazed. Calmly and gently, he wiped his arm with sterile gauze.

Perhaps Bri's friends had been right: the craggy, abrasive creature she'd experienced these past few weeks wasn't the real Ian.

Ian refused to react to the sting of Bri's nails. She was anxious, hurting and stressed, so her actions were understandable.

Odd, though, her latching onto him for comfort so easily. Especially since he'd been a total jerk to her for weeks.

Not liking the claws of guilt scraping at him, Ian adjusted Bri's IV drip and faced Kate, jotting

Bri's vitals. "She needs antibiotics, trauma labs, X-rays and CTs stat."

Kate nodded. They effortlessly hefted the backboard to the gurney and push-ran Bri, who was so tall her heels almost hung off the end.

Kate's cell chimed. Without missing steps, she answered. "Hey, wanna start this way? Ian needs to cut out and we have an incoming ladder mishap. Yeah. Lodge owner next door."

"Lisa, my nurse anesthetist." Ian couldn't miss this court hearing. Yet he couldn't leave Bri. Her condition could skid off a cliff without warning. Eighty percent of people falling from heights of eleven feet or more died. She'd fallen nine. Internal injuries didn't always present right away.

He'd learned that the hard way, overseas while deployed with Mitch, Kate and other air force trauma-team members who had yet to join them at EPTC, Mitch's stateside endeavor.

"Why would I need an *anesthes*—that thing?" Bri swallowed.

Ian glanced down, resisting the urge to rest a calming hand on hers. "In case the need arises to surgically repair your arm."

She had no clue that could be the least of her worries. Part of his job, for now, was to keep her clueless. If she were bleeding internally, increased anxiety could speed her pulse, hasten hemorrhage and put her life at risk.

"The break is bad, isn't it?" Dread crinkled her forehead. "How soon can I use my arm?"

Ian's determination sparked. "Only after it's healed."

Bri tensed and licked her lips. "And when will that be?"

Inside EPTC, they wheeled Bri into a trauma bay. "Depends on if soft tissue is involved or just bone. Six weeks minimum."

"Six week—" Choked on the words, Bri tried to sit up. Kate restrained her. "I'll never make the deadline!"

She must mean foreclosure proceedings. Caleb had filled Ian in. Bri's face strained as he studied her. Sensing her struggle, Ian squeezed her shoulder reassuringly, then stepped out. Simple gesture. Sincere. Yet it seemed to make her want to cry more.

He wished he could help, but he had his own stuff going on. Deadlines from every direction. Work, plus training, plus helping set up a second trauma crew so EPTC didn't lose vital funding.

Then there was Tia, his only daughter and number one priority. She should have been all along, but a mentally unstable mother and a cross-continental war had caused him to be a stranger in his daughter's eyes.

Ian's gut clenched. Sweat misted his palms. If he didn't show in court today, that could put him in jeopardy with the judge who would decide Tia's fate and their future as a family.

He eyed his watch, and hoped Lisa would get here soon or he'd be faced with abandoning a patient and breaking a battlefield promise to a brother-in-arms. Stress drove him to walk halls.

After pacing, Ian parked his anesthesia cart outside Bri's bay. Regret multiplied. He'd promised Caleb to watch over her. He'd failed. He owed Caleb. Big-time. Ian reentered Bri's room, intent on righting his wrong. "You hangin' in there, Bri?"

Not until seeing her under fluorescent lighting did he realize how white-blond and silky long her hair was. Blinking swiftly, she aimed her pretty cornflower-blue eyes up at him, making him momentarily forget what he came in here for. Must be lack of sleep from a week's worth of on-call nights. "Dr. Shupe, what turned me too stupid to heed Caleb's warning?"

He wanted to chuckle. "It's Ian. And trust me, my list of stupid things is twice as long as yours. Kate's is triple."

Kate snorted from the corner of the room and stepped out. Bri's face sobered. "Seriously, what stripped my common sense today?"

"Could be the ominous bank notices you've been getting recently."

She stared long and hard at him. "You know about that?"

He nodded. Bri lost the battle holding in her tears the second Kate came in carrying X-rays and a sympathetic expression. "Sorry, Bri. The bones aren't aligned, so surgery is a must."

Ian knew that could double her recovery time and triple her chances of losing the lodge. Compassion for Bri and Caleb washed over Ian. They had just lost their mom and were about to lose their childhood home and heritage. Not to mention the community was about to lose an iconic retreat center that once was, according to Mitch, the bustling pulse of the rustic, close-knit community.

The bank had planned to shut down and level the Landis family's grounds, which included the main lodge, fourteen cabins and seven bunkhouses.

His morning runs around Eagle Point Lake revealed the retreat as a flat horizontal triangle. The main lodge made the point, seven cabins on either side angled out in two lines and bunkhouses formed a bottom line opposite the lodge.

"Bri, if you're worried about losing the lodge, don't be."

Surprise flashed across her face. Tears welling up meant he'd hit a nerve. "Your cabins need to be fixed. I worked construction in college. Let me help."

"I don't accept anything for free."

"You can't be serious?" The stubborn set to her jaw said she was. "Fine. Caleb mentioned you have a child-care degree. I need a permanent sitter for Tia. Problem solved."

"You mean, like a barter?"

"That's exactly what I mean. Think about it."

The next moments were a flurry of activity as Bri was assessed, prodded, questioned, medicated, primped with surgical garb and prepped.

Ian smiled at her. Her vitals had calmed after he'd proposed the barter. It could work. He'd just have to be brutal with his time, which meant no entertaining, no socializing and definitely no dating.

Lisa rushed up, tying her mask. "I'm here, Ian. Shoo. Go."

Bri hyperventilated at the O.R. doors. Understandable, since, according to Caleb, their mom died in surgery. Ian brushed fingers along Bri's hand. She clutched him in a death grip. "Please don't tell Caleb I broke my arm. I'm scared it'll distract him in combat. I can't lose another family member. He's all I have." Her raw voice disintegrated.

That she was more concerned for her brother than for herself hit Ian to the core.

He held on to her fingers as long as he could. He was already late for court, and her orthopedic surgeon waited not so patiently. But Bri's pleading eyes *really* got to him.

But, he *had* to get to court.

He also had to call her brother. If she had complications in surgery or under general anesthesia, they'd need directives from family. She'd be mad, but being a doctor wasn't a popularity contest. It meant making hard decisions that sometimes caused pain. He averted his gaze.

"Ian, Caleb can't know I'm in surgery. Okay?"

Despite the risk of making her angry by disregarding her request, Ian was convinced Caleb needed to know. Ian released Bri's fingers and nodded to Kate to take her on in.

Even out of sight, Bri's pleading face wouldn't leave his mind. He sighed. Rounded the corner. Walked the hall. He pulled out his phone, knowing legally, ethically and morally, he had to call her emergency contact. He hoped it would be a nonissue.

Especially when Bri discovered he'd called her brother.

Caleb was a capable army medic. He could handle hard information and compartmentalize it in a way to keep his head in the game and not endanger himself or his fellow soldiers.

On the other hand, if something happened to Caleb…

Ian weighed his options, waffling between Bri's atypical emotional plea and what his doctors' creed dictate he do.

Ian sighed. This time at the irony of staring at a so-called smart phone while wondering if this would turn out to be the stupidest thing he had ever done.

His Hippocratic oath came to mind. But doubt assailed him. Her surgery was dangerous and she had no one else to call. Caleb had confided that their estranged dad was incapacitated in a nursing home. A sense of sadness over her isolation riddled Ian.

Nevertheless, he pulled up the number for Caleb's commander, texted a message marked as urgent and pushed Send.

The morning after surgery, Bri woke from a groggy mist to a most pleasant sound. A masculine voice drawing close. A deep chuckle, then, "Get some sleep, Kate."

Ian? Bri's eyes fluttered open at the smell of evergreen. Ian's cologne reminded her of Christmas. He approached and rested casual elbows on her bed's side rail. "Good morning, Crash."

A smile touched her lips before she could stop it. She took in Ian's disheveled appearance.

Wrinkled scrubs. Ruffled hair. Sleepy eyes and a shadow-roughed jaw she hoped he wouldn't shave. "You look worse than I feel," she fibbed. "Rough night?"

Lip twitching, he ripped an O.R. mask off his neck. "Yeah. The shortest day of the year feels like infinity."

"That's right. Today's the first day of winter." She also recalled the barter. "Were you serious yester—"

Rock music chimed. Annoyance flashed across his face as if it were the call coming across his touch screen. Ian's reaction made her courage disappear, taking her back to intimidating tones Eric had used when she'd unwittingly called at "inconvenient" times.

Ian touched his cell phone. "Shupe."

"Ian, this is your neighbor," said an older woman. "I want to make you aware your little'n wandered over here again."

Ian's face snapped up, his expression full of worry. "Tia's there?"

"Yes. I'm guessing your babysitter got too busy texting again to realize Tia was gone. Again."

Ian's jaw rippled. "I'll be there right away, Miss Ellie."

"I'd watch her for you, but I've got chemo today."

"No, no, Ell. You *need* to keep your appointment." His voice, tender upon first hearing Ell's voice, softened more.

Suddenly realizing Bri had heard the entire conversation, Ian masked his features and stepped out.

His child care wasn't working out and he was considering a leave from EPTC, which opened mere months ago. His absence would strain staff and halt expansion projects. She knew about those from small-town breakfast chatter at Sully's, a local mom-and-pop eatery.

Also, Mitch, EPTC's founder, requested prayers at Eagle Point Lake Pavilion's "PRAYZ" gathering Tuesday, a weekly event Lauren and Kate had invited Bri to attend. Bri had learned there of Ian's struggles with Tia, whose mom had abandoned her. Bri had her own wounds from when her father had left them destitute. Like her neurotic inability to accept help.

Would Ian be angry if he knew people prayed for him? Eric had gone ballistic upon discovering she confided in praying pals about their faltering relationship. She'd been foolish to let him bully her into staying together. Never again would she let a man intimidate and manipulate her with angry words and arctic moods.

Ian exited an office across the hall and reentered her room. He grabbed his lab coat off a wall hook, brusque motions depicting the strain of a struggling single dad who hadn't gotten enough sleep in the two weeks Tia had been living with him. He stormed for the door, then doubled back.

He snatched a parent how-to book off her chair, evidence he'd been here before. Her gaze sought his. Face stony, he crammed the book under his arm. Why hide it? No one blamed him for wanting to be a better dad. He left in a stiff, half-hearted daze.

Fifteen minutes later, the sound of a little girl crying pierced Bri's heart. "I don't wanna come here! I want my mom!"

Ian passed by with a tiny flailing person clad in a purple tutu. His face and bulky arms were severely strained, and the child was crying like a banshee. "I want my mo-o-om!"

But your mom doesn't want you.

Bri knew that from town chatter, too—that Ian fiercely shielded Tia from her mom's rejection.

"I don't *want* you! I don't *know* you!" Tia screamed at Ian.

"I know, Tia. I'm sorry," Ian said, his voice raw but gentle. "But I know and love you. Things will end up all right. I promise."

Bri hoped Ian believed his own words. But while his voice was calm and confident, his eyes were desperate.

Thankfully, Tia couldn't see. Her face was red, and her cries gradually softened to hiccuppy whimpers.

Ian walked the floor with Tia swaddled in the strength of his arms. He swayed her, feet bouncing in gentle rhythmic daddy-dance Bri hoped Tia would recognize as his way of infusing security and comfort. Bri's heart squeezed.

How could she complain about her own problems when fragile Tia was in such harrowing turmoil? Bri's heart broke for the little girl.

Lord, mend this broken family. Help Tia trust her daddy. Help her daddy trust You. Prove to them You Are.

The next time Ian passed, Tia rested a chafed and soppy cheek against his broad shoulder. Ian's tenderness melted Bri.

Wow. He wasn't the icy-hearted guy she thought she knew. Bri strained to see past shadows muting her view. Emotion glimmered in his eyes. He didn't look as though he had strength left to care who saw it, either. Though Ian's brooding insolence reminded Bri of Disney's Beast, she'd help them for Tia's sake.

Kate entered with Bri's bone surgeon, who examined her, wrote discharge orders and left. Kate handed Bri a gift bag.

"Clean clothes!" Bri's heart swelled at the gesture. Kate helped her dress around the cast. "Um, is Ian still here?"

"I'll send him in." As Kate stepped out, she smirked.

Ian walked in, looking worn and weary, moments later. "Kate's watching Tia so you can speak with me. What's up?"

Bri's nerves coiled like a Slinky. "About that barter. We're still on, right?"

Ian smiled like a sunrise. "You're sure?"

"Absolutely. Bring Tia tomorrow morning, in fact."

His gaze tacked across her casted arm. "Not sure that's—"

"My surgeon said I could still train for the fundraising marathon. If I can run a 5K race, I can chase a kindergarten-bound kid."

"'Chase' is right." His face sharpened. Eyes narrowed. "How did you know her age and that she's starting school next year?"

"Uhm, I—" she stammered. "It's a small town. People talk, Ian."

His mouth thinned. "Apparently."

"So, about that barter…"

"You'll let me help renovate the lodge, no resistance?"

"None. You save my cabins from foreclosure. I solve your child-care problem." She reached out her hand. "Deal?"

He hesitated, then shook guardedly, nodding to her cast. "Deal. So long as you don't overdo it and undo the repairs we did."

"We?"

He scrubbed his neck. "Yeah. I, uh, scrubbed in for your surgery."

"Why? It's not like my injuries were life threatening."

His silence unnerved her, and negated her statement.

"Thanks, Ian. That was nice of y—"

"It's my job," he responded too quickly. She opted not to inform him he wasn't convincing. She stuffed her feet into her shoes and realized she couldn't tie them one handed.

He knelt and did it for her without her having to ask.

Bri bristled and cringed. She hated to be the one needing help.

"Thanks. By the way, the really caring guy I glimpsed on the asphalt yesterday? Then today in the hall hoisting a princess in poufy purple? I hope he sticks around awhile."

Chapter Two

Ian hoped this wasn't a mistake.

He was who he was, and that was that. Appeasing Bri wasn't a priority. Yet, here he was, trekking to her house with Tia.

Coyotes howled in the dusky morning distance. Not distant enough for his liking. He put himself between the woodlands and Tia as they crossed a forest-flanked parking lot between the ritzy state-of-the-art trauma center and Bri's humble log home. Another feral round of howls sounded. He reached for Tia.

She jerked away, pink tutu fanning her jeans. "I don't want to hold your hand and I *don't* wanna go to her icky tree house."

Ian stopped. Eyed Bri's place. Icky? Hardly. Tree house? He smiled. Tia had obviously never seen a log home before. It *did* look pioneerish under the effect of a purple twilight.

"Tia, I *have* to be in surgery with my patient in twenty minutes." He gritted his teeth and ignored the guilt.

A newborn winter breeze rustled Tia's curly brown hair and caused it to fall over her amber-eyed scowl. As they passed the luminous main lodge and approached Bri's cabin, Tia got busy in bribe mode. "Please-don't-make-me-go!" came out as one word. Her face brightened. "I'll even clean my room."

Ian dipped his head to hide the snicker. Truth be told, her offer tempted, since this morning her room had turned into a disaster. How could one small person make that big a mess? "Tell you what, we'll get Sully's sherbet after work."

"I don't like ice cream. And I don't like *you!*" She shoved him away, looking like a fugitive pondering flight. He pinched the hem of the new coat he'd bought her in case she made good on the getaway brewing in her eyes. Bri must've heard the sidewalk scuffle, because she peeled her window curtain back.

Ian knelt in front of Tia, who glared at him. "Clearly, you're not happy about having to come here. But I need your cooperation. Please, mind Miss Bri, and be careful of her arm."

Bri stepped onto a rambling redwood deck that shone with a new coat of cherry lacquer she must've applied. Ian stood.

Tia went ballistic, eyes darting around the tree-dotted yard as though seeking escape. Panic filled him that she might actually pull it off. His eyes veered to the deep lake. Images of last night's river drowning victims flooded Ian's imagination. He bent down, embarrassed he didn't know this yet about his own daughter. "Tia, how well do you swim?"

"I don't know. I never tried it." She eyed the sparkly sapphire lake, looking very much as though she wanted to, though. Fear like Ian had never known noosed his neck.

Bri knelt. "I'll make sure she doesn't leave my sight," she reassured as though seeing the stark fear swirling inside him. Ian had never known fire-red, dragon-breathing fear. Not even in combat.

This was his daughter. His joy. His life.

If something were to happen to her...

Ian swept her up in his arms and hugged tight despite her wriggling and making gagging noises. A kiss planted on her forehead, he carried her inside Bri's cabin and set her down at the farthest end from the lake and all its dangers. "I'll be back at two. Sooner if I can. Later if traumas pour in."

Ian felt hope as Tia darted behind his legs, away from Bri. He knelt at eye level, bracing Tia's arms. "Listen, Miss Bri is your new babysitter. She's fun. You'll like her."

She scowled at him, then Bri. "I'll *hate* her."

"Not acceptable, Tia." Beyond that, he didn't know what to say. Make her apologize? He could crawl under a rock. As a dad, he was an epic failure. He studied Tia, hoping for a lightning bolt of wisdom.

Bri knelt in front of Tia. "You mean to tell me you'd *hate* a babysitter who *loves* to fairy hunt?"

Tia's eyes widened. Anger fled. Flabbergasted, Ian blinked. What just happened here?

"Fairy hunt?" Tia sucked in a heap of air. "For *real?*" She looked at Ian for confirmation.

"Sure," he answered Tia. "Bri's a renowned fairy hunter."

Suspicion narrowed Tia's eyes. She stepped over to Bri. Aimed a finger at her nose. "Prove it."

When Bri rose, extending her arm, Tia reached for her hand.

And just like that, Bri won his daughter's fragile trust.

A little jealous, Ian bid them goodbye with his daughter's demand ringing through his head and heart.

Prove it.

Those two words were the summation of his life right now, Ian thought as he strode a familiar path to the trauma center.

He desperately needed to win Tia's trust.

Needed to prove he wasn't the world's biggest failure as a husband and a dad. Prove to a bank that Bri's lodge was worth saving. Prove to financial backers that his trauma center expansion projects were worth their time and dime. And lastly, he needed to know, and needed Tia to know, that life would get better. That she'd be okay.

Especially since the ink had dried on unpreventable papers. Ones on which Tia's mom had too easily signed her away. Anger consumed him that Ava chose a sleazy boyfriend over a child. Now at EPTC's side entrance for employees, he jerked open the heavy steel door, stormy gray like his mood. He stalked down the halls, not caring that staff had to scramble out of his way.

He wanted to get these surgeries over with and end this too-long and terrible day. Get back to his daughter and try to earn the trust that would take all her pain away.

The second Ian stepped into the operating room, he became all about the medicine. His focus fastened fully on the patient. A patient who deserved a better bedside manner than Ian had displayed walking in here.

A teen girl with the same color hair as his daughter's.

He needed to apologize to his staff and resist making excuses for his bad behavior. Sure, he'd been up all night tending a never-ending stream of traumas. Hard ones. The kind he couldn't save. But so had they. Friday nights were like that.

At the operating table, he faced Mitch. "We need to come up with some positive activities for teens around here, bro. Alcohol-infested parties sent way too many of 'em in here last night." And two of them to their graves prematurely.

Mitch nodded and began to work on the teen whose face had fractured on impact from projectile wine-cooler bottles last night. Two unbelted passengers had been ejected and pulled massive amounts of water into their lungs when the car skidded into a riverbank.

Ian fought worrying over Tia and her curiosity, and Bri's cabin sitting so close to the lake. Ian trusted Bri. He focused on damping down his fear while enabling his patient to breathe. "She owes her life to her seat belt. It's good she was buckled, but she shouldn't have had access to alcohol at age sixteen."

Mitch nodded. "Agreed."

A series of mechanical beeps, shooshes and stainless-steel-on-steel chinks invaded the sterile suite along with silent concentration as the surgery got under way.

After their successful operation, Ian found Mitch charting at a mahogany desk in the plaid-decor doctors' lounge. "Did you hear what I said earlier about creating alternatives for teens?"

Mitch scratched notes on a post-op report and sighed. "I'll stick it on the list." Remorse flickered in his eyes. "I hate being so time strapped." He was getting married in a few months. While Ian was happy for Mitch, attending his wedding was going to be difficult. Especially in light of a divorce Ian had desperately tried to prevent.

Plus, they were under a ton of pressure to get a second trauma crew selected and trained so the current crew wasn't so stretched with long hours and lack of sleep. Like last night.

Poor Tia. He'd had to drag her here. *Tia!* Ian slammed his watch up. Ten past two. He stood abruptly. "Hey, Mitch, catch you later. Gotta go. I promised Tia I'd try and be back by two." He sprinted across EPTC's lot, past Landis Lodge to Bri's cabin, hoping her quirky bird clock hadn't squawked, alerting Tia to his lateness.

Bri met his approach at the deck, finger to her lips. He tripped with a tremendous clatter over a gnome in her yard. Despite winter's chilly onset, heat blasted his neck.

After seeing if he was okay, Bri bit back a grin and stood. "Try to be quiet. She's napping."

"Wow. You got her to nap?" He stepped into her cabin to mouthwatering scents of Italian herbs, roasted tomatoes and cheesy pasta. The open-room layout afforded a great view of her forest-critter themed kitchen and stove. His stomach growled, reminding him he'd been too occupied to eat.

"We hunted fairies all morning." She motioned him to have a seat and set a tall glass of tea in front of him.

He sipped, loving the memories it evoked of dinners with family. A scenario Bri probably hadn't experienced in years. His heart clenched, wondering if it would always be just him and Tia.

He'd missed family get-togethers while at war. He needed to carve out time to take Tia to visit his mom. She'd like Bri. Ian ripped his gaze from whatever culinary goodness bubbled in that pan, and the ridiculous notion that Bri would ever meet his mom.

Bri watched him. Too carefully. "Would you and Tia like to have dinner with me?"

He rubbed the condensation on his glass. "I guess we could." His stomach rumbled intense gratitude. "What time?"

"How does five sound?"

"Great, actually. That'll give me a couple hours to wrangle the cabin that bucked you off its roof." He smirked and reached for a washed cherry tomato she'd put in a bowl. The second he popped it in his mouth, his tongue cheered. "I'm kinda hungry."

"I kinda noticed." Bri grinned. "We'll see you at five."

Ian jogged past the trauma lot to Lakeview Road, where his yard sat two houses away from EPTC. He loaded work stuff in his truck and drove to Bri's, not wanting Tia to have to trek home in the dark. Once there, he attacked cabin renovations with fervor.

A little over two hours later, his cell rang. "Hey, Bri."

"Hi. Wanted to let you know dinner's almost ready. Also, Tia's still sleeping. She's not feverish, so I don't think she's ill. But I wasn't sure how long you wanted her to nap. Any longer and she's liable not to sleep well tonight."

If he got called in again, Tia wouldn't sleep well, anyway. "Go ahead and let her sleep. I'll grab a shower and be over."

Her hesitation jabbed him. He needed more regular hours, but that couldn't happen until they got a second trauma crew trained. Ian sprinted home, showered and walked back to Bri's. The second she let him in, his taste buds watered in anticipation. "It smells amazing."

So did she, as she leaned close to him to refresh his glass. "Vanilla?"

Her eyes rose. "No, just plain old tea."

"I meant your perfume. It's nice. So is the tea." He inhaled the iced tea in two gulps. "Iced, even in winter?" he added since she shifted uncomfortably under his compliment. Best to keep things casual. Not personal.

"It's Southern Illinois. People sit in hot tubs and drink sweet iced tea all year round, even on cool nights."

"I can believe that." He stretched his back and arms.

Her gaze skittered over him, then quickly away, eyes like a feather across his skin. She pulled out burgundy-cushioned bar stools at the kitchen counter dividing a warm-umber dining room from the canary-yellow kitchen. Her color choices were like the varying levels of her personality: shy but strong, bright and stark, each wall painted a different vivid, modern color.

Unlike his walls, which were a mix of muted, neutral, dark and subdued, which matched his personality right now.

For a brief second, Ian wished Bri knew the humorous, lighthearted, fun-loving guy he used to be. Then his marriage had imploded. Life would never be the same and he'd likely never be that guy again. Her words drifted back: *That guy? I hope he sticks around.* For the first time in a long time, Ian did, too.

But workload, stress and the pain of divorce didn't promise to let up anytime soon, so it was doubtful.

Bri motioned him to a stool, then sat on one herself.

He eased onto the end stool, leaving two comfortably between them. He enjoyed the break on his feet. He'd been on them nearly twenty-six hours now. "Find any fairies today?"

She chuckled, lowering her gaze. Her lashes brushed the high slope of her cheek. "No, but the troll you tripped so gracefully over has been assigned by Tia to scout the yard for them."

"I see. I'm not surprised Tia napped, actually. I had to drag her out of bed twice to bring her to the trauma center."

She shifted thoughtfully. "How come? Did you get called in on a case or something?" She swiped a bead of tea off her lip.

He averted his gaze. "Yeah. Twice." He should reassure her Tia hadn't been unattended. Passed around amid nurses, yes. Left alone for one minute, no. "Staff took turns watching her."

She adjusted her arm sling. "That won't work long-term."

Ian nodded, feeling fortunate to have Bri babysitting. She cared. "At least Tia's not being shuffled around during the daytime, thanks to you."

Still, no wonder Tia's moodiness had escalated this morning. She hadn't had proper sleep. Bri was right. It couldn't last. He was her only parent now. "I need to establish a routine and propagate proper sleep."

A smile touched Bri's lips.

"At least that's what that bossy parenting book said."

That made her laugh. He was glad. More than he should be.

He forced the smile back down. "I'd like to tell the book's know-it-all author his ridiculous creative parenting ideas are easier said than done for time-strapped single parents in survival mode."

She rubbed her arm above the cast. "What creative ideas?"

"Silly stuff, like making Christmas trees with stacked star cookies and caterpillars out of cupcakes and—"

She jerked. Eyes darted to the counter behind him. He turned, peering at the artistic culinary creations, including none other than a caterpillar cupcake.

He looked at Bri. Face down, she rubbed her arm again. Two things greatly concerned him. One, she seemed fearful he'd ridicule her for the cutesy cupcakes she and Tia had created. Second, she couldn't seem to leave her arm alone.

"You keeping up with your pain meds, Bri?"

Her eyes veered even farther away. Yet the stubbornness befell her that Caleb had warned him about. "As much as possible. I don't want to risk falling asleep with Tia here."

"Aw, Bri. I considered that. You need—"

Her head shook. "No. I'm tough. I can take a little pain."

She might have convinced him had the hollowness not haunted her eyes. She rose swiftly and went to work at the stove.

Ian followed, grabbing salad ingredients. "You okay?"

She shrugged. "I'm worried about Caleb. He hasn't called."

Ian froze, knife midslice in a cucumber. Come to think of it, he hadn't heard from Caleb, either. Not since the day of Bri's surgery. "I'll call him. Find out what's going on."

Bri added carrots to the lettuce Ian tossed. "No, let me. I'm afraid if you call him, you'll tell him about my injury."

Bri grew alarmed when Ian tensed. "He doesn't know, right?"

Tia must've woke because she shuffled in the next room. "Yes! I'm *sure* of it, Boom. They got hillbilly fairies in this here forest. And it's not only haunted with fairy-eating trolls, it's naked. All the PJs blew to the ground, Boom."

Ian and Bri turned. Tia walked circles, play phone to her bed-head ear. *Naked?* The fairies or the forest? Bri wondered.

"How odd," Ian said, watching Tia wear tracks on the wood parquet floor Bri had installed last week. At least she'd gotten her cabin renovated before falling, thus had a decent place to live.

"What's odd? Boom? He's Tia's imaginary friend."

He scowled. "She's my daughter. I am well acquainted with Boom, the infamous scapegoat for Tia's messy room. I meant odd in the sense that I pace like that when I'm on my cell phone."

Bri felt like laughing at the fact that Ian didn't seem the least bit alarmed by Tia's talk of ill-attired fairies, fallen PJs or cannibalistic trolls. Yet at the same time, Bri's ire rose at being scolded over explaining who Boom was.

She drew a deep breath to calm down. "I noticed her pacing. And you never answered my question about Caleb."

His eyes flicked to her with annoyance before returning to rest on Tia. The look of wounded nostalgia entering his eyes caused Bri to stop pressing the Caleb issue. For now.

Ian might be standing here now but his mind was a world away. He watched Tia with a mix of regret and awe as she paced like he did. "I wonder what else she acquired from me," he said, confirming Bri's hunch.

"She definitely acquired your beastly moods and appetite."

Before Ian could utter a retort, Bri stepped out of his line of fire. "Tia, wash your hands. Dinner's ready." Bri went to pull garlic bread from the oven.

Ian blocked her. "Let me." He eyed her casted arm. "You could get burned." His gaze bore down on her, squelching any protest. Burned? Felt as if she already was.

He neared to help set the table. "You need to trust me."

She whirled. "About my arm? Or Caleb?"

A muscle clicked in his jaw. "Both."

"I'm sorry, Ian. I hate not knowing if he'll be okay and I hate being in the humbling position of needing help." Bri clenched her teeth against urges to confront more about Caleb.

Both men being tight-lipped could mean Caleb was about to embark on a mission of danger she'd be better off oblivious to. "FYI, Tia also acquired your rude penchant toward ignoring, hedging and projecting in order to protect your secrets."

Tia "hung up" her play phone and skipped into the kitchen, unaware of her dad's gaping mouth. Well, what did he expect? He'd been harsh with his words and truth, too.

They sat at the big, rustic wood table that had been Mom's. Despite the tension, dinner started out light and fun and lively but ended subdued with Ian growing more withdrawn and sullen. So much so, Bri jumped when her wall screeched like a pterodactyl.

Humor hit Ian's eyes as he studied her, then the bird clock above the fireplace mantel that held copious pictures of Caleb,

"Stupid clock. It's too loud. Caleb got it for me for Christmas last year as a source of torment. I can't get rid of the obnoxious thing, because despite its screeching bird sounds, it's sentimental."

Ian almost smiled. "Hard to believe Christmas is three days away. What are your plans?"

She shrugged. "Probably eat a frozen turkey dinner and watch Hallmark movies."

"I've had no time for TV lately."

His eyes veered toward Tia, their color deepening to a dark blue, like a stormy sky. "A teen girl almost perished last night. She looked like I'd imagine Tia will in ten years. Identical hair, down to the natural ringlet curls."

"I bet that was hard," Bri said.

The vulnerable look entering his eyes next caught her completely off guard. He rose and brushed aside Bri's ruffled maroon curtains. Thoughtfully eyed the main lodge through Bri's big side window. "Do you have plans for the big lodge?"

She joined him at the window. "Yeah. Mom's dreams."

He faced her, his expression softening to a point that she had to look away. She felt too vulnerable otherwise. "Mom would hold sewing, cooking and quilting classes for her church ladies. She wanted to open it up to the community. She died before her dreams came true." Bri shrugged the chill away.

Ian eyed her shoulders, then moved toward her but stopped.

Had he been about to come behind her and rub her arms?

"I have an idea, if you want to hear it," he said.

Bri laughed. "Since when do you ever ask permission to share your opinion or waylay anyone daring to disagree with it?"

He smirked. "Point taken. The accident was fatal for two other teens. Alcohol was a factor. That lodge would be a very cool hangout for teens. You should consider letting me and Mitch fix it up as such once he gets some time."

"It would give them something safe to do. There's a big area downstairs that would be perfect for pool tables, a digital arcade, even laser tag. I could use the upstairs rooms for corporate events and meetings."

"And those classes your mom started." Ian smiled kindly.

"It's a great idea, Ian. But I'd be remiss to let you and Mitch do it. You're already renovating my cabins. I saw where you'd cleared the ivy away and replaced the gutters. Thanks."

He nodded. "You're helping me in a big way, too. With Tia."

Bri peered once more at the lodge. Longing took root. "I'd hate to infringe on your time like that."

"There's nothing more important to me than saving lives, Bri." He cast a glance over at Tia. "She'll be a teen someday."

Bri caught the fear in his words. "Trust God, Ian."

He faced her. "I did. Once. My marriage crumbled, anyway. I lost my wife long before the divorce, Bri. She bailed when I gave my life to God and she didn't want to."

"I'm sorry, Ian. That must have been hard—"

"Boom wants in on the sherbet," Tia announced loudly from the puppet box she'd dived into after dinner.

Ian approached and picked up a fox puppet. "Tell Boom if he can eat sherbet, he can help clean Tia's room."

Tia's face popped out of the puppet stage curtain. She pointed sideways. "He's right here."

Tia glared at her dad. "Tell him yourself, Mister Meanie Fox who takes baby rabbits away from their mothers."

Tia wore bunny ears and a matching cottontail.

Ian's jaw clenched.

Bri didn't miss the pain Tia's words had lashed across his eyes. Bri tensed like a witness to a car wreck.

Flashes of Eric's rage at his nephew spilling a shake in his Corvette came to mind. Then how her ex had railed her all the way to the car wash for "stupidly inviting the kid along."

But Ian didn't blow. He calmly pulled the fox puppet off his arm. Set it in the box. Knelt face-to-face with his daughter. Love never left his eyes. "Tia, I know it's hard when things change and we don't want them to. But that doesn't mean we can leave someone's home a mess."

"Ours could sparkle clean and it would *still* be a mess. You don't do *anything* right. Not bedtime stories or bath time or eggs or Christmastime or nothing! Especially your icky eggs! And your animal pancakes are stupid! They don't look like air force aardvark fairies at all!"

"Aardvark fairies?" Bri blurted before she could think.

"Yes. They fly in and eat all the bugs." She glared again at Ian. "He has ants in his house and I *hate* living there. We don't even have a tree or cookies and Santa is coming in—" Rant paused, she counted on her fingers and gasped. "Three days!"

Ian looked about to scold Tia for speaking disrespectfully, but his cell phone rang. He viewed the screen. Relief hit his face.

"Excuse me." He carried plates to the sink with one hand and answered his call with the other. He went to Bri's deck to speak, eyes flitting her way through a window.

Bri put leftovers away. "Tia, let's get toys picked up."

"Can you go to Sully's with us?" Tia asked as they worked.

"Um, well…" She didn't want to barge in on daddy-daughter time. Plus, her arm was *really* hurting.

Tia grabbed Bri's good hand and squeezed. "Please?"

Ugh. She was a heartbreaker, this kid. Bri eyed Ian, who walked in with a neutral expression. Too neutral. "Was that Caleb?" Bri pegged.

"Yes. He's fine. Said to tell you he loves you but not to call. He'll be out of range for three weeks. He'll call you—and me—when he's back at base."

She gritted her teeth, and felt as if she was the only one not in on the full conversation.

Bri fought hurt that Caleb didn't speak to her

and that Ian didn't encourage him to. Why? Was Ian as thoughtless as Eric? Or was Caleb imminently marching into more serious combat danger?

"Miss Bri's going to Sully's with us," Tia announced.

Bri stiffened, ready for Ian's explosion. Eric never liked when his pals had included Bri in their get-togethers.

The only thing that ignited on Ian's face was a smile. "Awesome. Tia, did you and Boom pick toys up?" Ian went to check the play area behind Bri's burgundy-and-blue-striped couch, leaving Bri to wonder why she tended to compare the two men.

It wasn't as if she was interested in Ian. She was simply becoming involved in his life because she was babysitting Tia. That was all.

Bri's unease had nothing to do with how handsome his jet-black hair looked in a fresh buzz. Or how his broad chest filled out a black leather jacket.

Nothing at all.

Chapter Three

Nothing at all was wrong with his heart. So why Ian's pulse skipped upon sight of a tall blonde jogging the lakeside trail ahead on his run the next morning, he had no idea. Especially since she resembled Bri. Platinum ponytail brushing her back with each athletic footfall, white wisps fluttering in the breeze, easy as her one-armed stride.

Wait. One arm? He sped up. Looked closer.

That *was* Bri.

Instant annoyance hit that he'd taken a second look.

"Hey, Crash!" he called so he wouldn't startle her by just running up next to her. "Cool the turbojets."

She turned and nearly tripped over a rut. Alarm sliced through him. He reached to steady her as they slowed. "Close call." He eyed the hot-pink cast that had given her away.

"Not as close as the goose who nearly took me out."

"It *is* called Gosling Way," he teased, referring to the walk-run trail adjacent to Duckshore Drive, which circled the water and led to Lakeview Road. It connected the trauma center and Landis Lodge to a residential area around Eagle Point Lake, where he and Mitch had homes built while overseas and planning this trauma center amid what felt like a million combat surgeries.

Bri's cheeks were red and her breathing labored enough he knew she'd been running awhile. "Where's T?" she huffed.

"Tia's still sleeping. Kate's watching her in the doctor's lounge for me."

Bri looked at him sharply. "At the trauma center?"

"Since I don't have a call room in my home, yes."

Bri veered off on the Gosling Way trail that led to Eagle Point Lake's pavilion behind EPTC. Ian followed, sensing she had something to say. Once she caught her breath, she pulled the lone iPod plug from her ear. That she only wore one and let the other dangle told him she was a serious runner, same as him.

"Still planning on the Library marathon?"

She nodded, and swigged water. "Yeah. You?"

"Yes. I'd be in trouble otherwise."

"That's right. I heard you helped Lauren's grandpa Lem organize it to fundraise for community projects."

"How'd you hear that?" He propped a foot on a concrete picnic table beneath the covered pavilion. It needed a new coat of paint. But like everything else in Eagle Point, money was tight, so upkeep of public parks suffered. Ian aimed to change that. If he was raising Tia here, he wanted it to thrive.

He realized Bri never answered. He leaned in.

She nibbled her lip. "Kate and Lauren organized a prayer and praise gathering here on Tuesday nights. They named it PRAYZ." Bri drew a fortifying breath, as if afraid to say the rest. "Mitch comes. He requests prayers for you and the trauma center a lot. He wants your fundraising efforts to succeed."

He eyed his watch. "I should get back. Tia will be waking soon." He turned back. "Be careful with your—"

"Arm. I know." She fell into step beside him, but for some reason all he wanted to do was get away. From her and the weird way it made him feel for people to air his personal life in public. And who prayed at a lake, anyway? Mitch, of course. Yet, he knew Mitch and his prayers were why Ian had made it through his divorce and deployments intact. He sighed. "Thanks for... never mind."

He wasn't convinced yet the prayers were working.

"Did you get called in again last night, Ian? You seem..."

"Beastly?" he bit out. Held her gaze and didn't dare let his face soften. "Yeah. Saturday nights are almost as bad as Friday with drunken accidents and parties. No one died, though."

"That's good."

"That's debatable."

She paused. "That means...?"

"The dad of the girl we saved is a private investigator. He checked around and found the guy who supplied the kids with alcohol. The P.I. first threw punches, then threw the guy out a second-story window. Now he's in jail." Ian smirked. "The offender who supplied underage kids with alcohol is in neck-to-ankle traction."

"Was that before or after EMS brought him in to you?"

Ian laughed, surprised by her humor. "Before."

She sighed. "We really need to get that teen hangout going. After the cabins, of course. And you *really* need to let me come to your house and watch Tia when you get called in."

At the trauma center lot now, he checked his

phone. Kate hadn't texted. He motioned Bri toward the lodge. "I'll walk you home and work on renovations until Kate texts me Tia's awake."

"Think about what I said, Ian. Your house is a four-minute jog from mine. But I can make it in two." She blushed. "I timed that route this morning. You have a beautiful place."

"You will, too, once the lodges are fixed up. You did a nice job with your personal cabin." Ian walked her to her door. "I'll be back with my truck in a bit."

He really wanted to run another lake lap, but that would take time he needed to get crackin' on Bri's second cabin.

He finished replacing windows when Kate called. "She awake?"

"Yes, but I need to borrow her for a few hours."

"Okay, what—"

"None of your beeswax. Christmas secrets."

"That'll give me time to get Tia's gift, too."

Kate scoffed. "You ruin everything, you big brute."

"I'll pretend to be surprised." A terrible feeling went through him. "Kate, don't be disheartened if, when you bring the whole buy-Daddy-a-present-thing up, Tia doesn't want to get me anything. She's still resentful and angry over her life being turned upside down. Right now, she considers me the enemy."

"Take heart, Ian," Kate said in childproof tones. "Tia is the one who brought it up. This was her idea. *She* asked *me* to take her."

Emotion throbbed behind Ian's eyes, and it took a second to compose himself. "Thanks, Kate." He hung up and turned.

Bri stood in her patchy yard with iced teas and a curious expression. He dipped his head so she wouldn't see evidence that he really wasn't all that strong. Aerosmith riffs blasted his phone again. Kate's camouflage monkey avatar lit the screen.

Had Tia changed her mind? Decided to give him nothing for Christmas except a hard time? He swiped the phone face. "Hey, Kate."

"Hey. Bri nearby?"

"Yeah, need to speak with her?"

"No. Walk nonchalantly away, out of her hearing range."

Kate never lost her military leader bossiness. Ever. "Okay, what's up?"

"At PRAYZ the other night, Bri casually mentioned not being able to shop and decorate her place for Christmas because of her arm. I think facing this first holiday without her mom has given her a case of the winter blues. She could use some holiday cheer. Take care of that for me? Like, today?"

"Sure." The sad thought dawned on Ian that,

if someone didn't intervene, Bri would be spending Christmas all alone. "You planning on taking Lem up on his invitation to come over and join him, Lauren, Mitch and a bunch of the pararescue jumpers for Christmas Eve dinner?"

"Yeah. You're not bailing on him, right?"

"No, actually, he'd mentioned to bring a friend if we wanted, that he'd have enough food to feed an army. Maybe we should invite Bri." Meaning maybe Kate would take it from here.

"Great idea, Ian. Let me know what she says when you ask."

"Wait—"

"Gotta run. Take your time shopping with Bri and have fun." She clicked off before he could formulate a coherent response.

The way Kate urged him to take his time, Ian got the distinct impression she was matchmaking him and Bri. He needed to disabuse her of that crazy notion.

Ian sighed at Bri's ramshackle cabins. If he was doing one a week, he needed help. "Time for backup," he told the curious woodland creature watching from a barren branch. The squirrel skittered up the tree. Ian smiled at Tia's depiction of trees that lose their leaves, aka *pajamas,* according to Tia—*pj's!*

Ian instantly thought of renovation recruits. A human PJ, though, not the cotton variety. "We're calling in air support," he informed the sniffing, bushy-tailed squirrel. "That bank doesn't stand a chance of leveling your home, little buddy."

He dialed Brockton Drake, the only unmarried holdout on a pararescue jumper—aka PJ—team stationed at Eagle Point Air Base near Refuge, a town away. The special operations skydiving paramedics helped at the trauma center sometimes to keep their medic skills up between combat and civilian rescues. Brock always told Ian to call if he needed anything. Today, he did. "Hey, Brock. What are you doing today?" Ian asked the hardworking air force PJ.

Whose pretty red truck is that? Bri watched it rumble past her cabin and park near the one Ian hammered on. Pausing her organizing of books for Lem's annual library fundraiser, she stepped onto her deck to see.

A strapping redheaded man with a bright smile and true military bearing exited the cab with construction supplies. Ian greeted him and together they unloaded wood from the truck bed.

Bri fought the urge to rush out and apologize for her shabby cabin. Yet the way the two men bantered back and forth, ribbing good-naturedly while working, suggested they didn't consider helping her an inconvenience. Ian laughed. It was such a rare occurrence, Bri smiled. She felt bad he was strapped to her cabin today when she wasn't watching Tia. Kate had volunteered to take her for a few hours of shopping.

The last time she'd asked Eric downstate to help her mom with the lodge so it wouldn't have to close, he'd scoffed. Told her he didn't have time for something so trivial.

The month away from him had made Bri see she'd be better off without him. He'd brainwashed her to believe she couldn't find a better guy. She stared at Ian. Was he a manipulator with moodiness, too? Bri rubbed the chill off her arms. Best get busy inside.

While the guys worked, Bri continued sorting mass amounts of books for Lem's annual library benefit. She had a hard time not cracking a book open and indulging.

Too tempted by the books, and sleepy from insomnia over worrying about Caleb, she set about sewing new curtains for each of the cabins. Seven cabins' worth later, a knock sounded at her door.

Ian and his pal stood on her landing.

"Hi, come on in. I was about to make lunch and bring you refreshments."

"I bragged on your tea," Ian said. "This is Brock, a buddy of mine from the Refuge side of Eagle Point Air Base."

"Nice to meet you, Brock." She shook his hand. "I'm Bri."

His dimples deepened as he smiled. "Ma'am." He eyed the floor. "Whoa. That's an avalanche of books." He bent down to peer at the titles. "Who reads all these?"

"I do. Ever since I was little, I've had an obsession with reading."

Ian poured tea in the two glasses she'd set down on the kitchen counter. He grabbed a third glass and filled it, too. "Join us on the deck?"

He handed her the glass and gestured. "Ladies first."

"Nice place," Brock commented, eyes gazing over the land.

"You should see it fixed up." Bri settled in the farthest seat across from Ian at the outdoor table.

"I will soon," Brock said, then passed Ian a look she couldn't decode.

Ian captured Bri's gaze. "You mentioned the bank's mandate to have seven financially stable renters by Valentine's Day. Pararescuemen on Brock's team are partnering with local first responders in rope rescue and other advanced training and conducting survival classes." He gestured behind her. "Those steep, silvery bluffs, deep lake, woodland terrain, caves and overgrown forests would make great training ground."

Brock leaned in. "Your cabins would be a great time-saver and give us a base close to the training area. I talked to my C.O., and Petrowski said to get info from you about renting a couple units. He said to tell you he'd be happy to send more recruits out to expedite the renovation process, if that would help."

Tears burned behind Bri's eyes. Relief, yes, but she hated embarrassing thoughts that two entire towns, Refuge and Eagle Point, plus an entire elite force of special ops airmen were conducting a conspiracy of kindness to help save her lodge. Because people in close-knit communities were like that.

Bri knew of the PJs. She'd had no idea Brock was one, but the way he carried himself—now she could see it. The PJs were famous in these parts and abroad. Esteemed and well respected. Honest. Superhero strong. Brave. Benevolent. A noble breed of valiant, honorable men who'd stand by their word or die. Men of integrity. Like Mitch, and—despite his brooding—Ian.

If she agreed to this, that meant three cabins had renters. Hers, and the two Brock inquired about. Yet, she wasn't paying. She needed to figure out how to generate more income. Kate had hinted about renting one of her cabins, but hadn't mentioned it since.

She must've been silent too long. Brock stood. "Think about it, ma'am. Get back to me, or Ian, whenever you've had a chance to come up with numbers. Money's not an issue for us, so charge what's comfortable for you."

She nodded, realizing with cautiously optimistic hope that, if things panned out right, renting the two cabins could both appease the bank and generate income to renovate the rest. Her money was quickly running out. She walked with Ian to accompany Brock to his truck despite Ian's hard face and formidable air.

Bri waved to Brock as he left. "Hope my silence didn't run him off."

"No, he told me earlier he had to get ready for HALOs tonight." Face still cast in a brooding light, Ian walked back to her deck and grabbed their glasses. He was so subdued she was compelled to help him thaw. *Talk to him.*

"HALOs?" She opened the kitchen door and they stepped in.

He met her attempts at conversation with a dark, pensive stare. It created such an atmosphere of danger, she took a step back. That snapped him out of it and seemed to alert him that he'd emanated a threatening impression.

He set the glasses in her sink and washed them. "High altitude, low opening. It's a special nighttime parachute jump from so high up, they have to have oxygen."

"Oxygen?" Her neck craned. "Nighttime?"

Ian grinned. "Yeah. Total blast."

"Maybe for you." She laughed cautiously, contemplating the thrill of free-falling. "I'd like to skydive someday. The *normal* way," she quickly tacked on. "When oxygen isn't required."

He brushed a finger along her arm. "After this heals, I'll take you. We could tandem jump until you feel safe to solo."

Right now, *solo* was the only thing that felt safe.

"At your own risk. I'm liable to blow out your eardrums."

Ian laughed. "Brock's team leader, Joel's wife, almost did the first time he took her." His grin faded, face pinched. "Not...that you're my wife— just—Caleb told me how adventurous you are."

"Told? Or *warned?*" She quirked an eyebrow at him, dried the glasses that had been Mom's and put them away, yet not memories of them standing at the lodge sink chattering over them. *Lord, I miss her so much.* Poor Tia. She had to miss hers, too. Chest tight, Bri drew a shaky breath.

Ian paused. Eyes went into assessment mode. "You okay?"

"Yeah. Christmas was Mom's favorite holiday is all."

"Hard." He brushed his thumb and forearm on her shoulder. While it was meant to be a touch of comfort, it left her skin feeling tingly.

"Speaking of Christmas, I wanted to take you

shopping today. I figured we could pick up some decorations and gifts. Grab a quick lunch here first and eat dinner while we're out?"

The thought of having holiday decorations ignited joy. The thought of having dinner with Ian made Bri cautious. Yet a sliver of excitement she didn't want to acknowledge grew within her. "I'd love that. Thank you, Ian."

He scratched his jaw and shifted from foot to foot. "Also, I was wondering if you'd like to join a few of us at Lem's for a Christmas Eve dinner tomorrow. Kate, Mitch and Lauren will be there, too. Plus Lem and Tia. We'd love to have you join us."

She sighed. Despite feeling like a pity case, Bri's former dread of spending Christmas alone and without Mom fled. "I heard Lem's Southern cooking is superb. If you're sure it's all right and that I won't be intruding, I'd love to go."

His face flashed with some undetectable emotion when she'd agreed to go. Was Ian happy she'd be going, or disappointed? She still found it difficult to read men's thoughts, because of her ex-boyfriend's changeable personality.

"Good. I'll pick you up at four since you can't drive yet." He walked over to the neatly stacked books. Then eyed the not-so-neat stack. "These for Lem's library fund and run?"

"Read-n-run." She giggled. "Yes.

"Need me to help you get them to Lem's place?"

"No, I—"

"Can't drive for six weeks. Let me rephrase—you hold open the door. I'll load these books into those plastic bins and we'll drop them off at the library on the way to the toy store."

She ground her teeth together. Resisted the temptation to inform him he was bossier than Kate. "Okay." While he loaded, she made pita sandwiches, which they ate before driving to town.

Partway through their excursion at Tinker's Toy Store in downtown Eagle Point, Bri indicated a fairy costume Ian held up with a raised brow. "Yes. Tia will love that."

"I hope so." Ian set the boxed dress-up ensemble in the cart and sighed dauntingly at the rows of other toys. "Did she happen to mention to you anything she'd like for Christmas?" He stuffed hands in his pockets. "I asked her, but she said the only thing she wants for Christmas is her mom." Ian's voice pinched.

Bri put a camouflage monkey in the cart. "For Kate."

Ian met Bri's gaze, and grinned like a slow dawn. "I never would have guessed. She's obsessed with those things."

Bri cleared her throat and kept stride with Ian

as he pushed the screechy cart. "Tia did mention a couple of things she wanted."

The squeaking wheels silenced as Ian paused the cart.

"She mentioned wanting a pet. Specifically a yellow dog, but if she can't have that, she'd settle for a fish named Jonah."

Ian's hands tightened around the cart. She tensed. "I'm frustrated she told you and not me."

"So, you'd consider a dog?"

"No. We don't have time to give it proper care and attention. The fish, however, is doable. If I can find a place to get one. I've been too busy to scout the town."

"That's partly my fault. And there's a pet store down the road." Bri pursed her lips. "I'll show you after we leave here."

Ian faced her. "Didn't mean to make you feel like a burden. Sometimes I don't think before I speak."

Sometimes? Bri bit her tongue from saying it. She needed to cool her jets and keep the peace. "I'm gonna look around."

Ian became subdued again "Fine. See you at checkout."

Fine? Like she needed his permission to shop. Ian was seeming more like domineering Eric every day. It was going to be tough to work as his babysitter, but she'd do it for Tia's sake, and for saving the lodge's sake.

Bri found a set of fairy books for Tia for Christmas and a gift card for Caleb, so he could load apps and games into his phone. Despite her anger, Bri added a second digital card for Ian when he wasn't at the checkout lanes. Where had he gone?

Two customers away from the cash register, Bri tried to open her wallet one handed. Couldn't. A strong hand pressed it back into her purse. She looked up. Ian stood behind her. He crammed a fistful of bills into her handbag. "What's that?"

"An advance on your paycheck."

Anger flashed. "I don't need your charity." She didn't want to make a scene, so she paid using his cash. Her fingers trembled, and her insides quivered as if they'd been set to broil. Someone as distinguished and well-off as Ian couldn't possibly understand why accepting handouts was so hard.

But she was about to let him have it.

Chapter Four

Ian's peripheral vision caught some motion happening at his car in the Tinker's Toys lot.

He turned around to see Bri whirling at him.

"Why did you do that?" Angry hurt flashed from her eyes.

Mind blank, he blinked. "Do what?"

She slammed her shopping bags into his open trunk. "Make people think I'm poor! Everyone saw the horrible thing you did!"

Was she kidding? What woman in her right mind would call two hundred free bucks horrible?

Ian couldn't help it. He burst out laughing.

That did not go over well. Fists balled and lips clenched, she got nose-to-chin with him. Few women could do that with his six-foot-four frame. She hissed through her teeth.

He partially turned, calmly dug the keys from his pocket and eyed her.

"I didn't know you had anger issues."

She shook her head. Threw the passenger door of his truck open and flung herself inside. "I don't have anger issues." She jabbed toward the street. "And the pet shop is that way."

"I didn't say you did. I'd like to know why you have a problem with people helping you. Had I known you'd be embarrassed, I'd have been more clandestine and considerate. I'm sorry."

Her shoulders relaxed, face calmed. "Unless you're up to your eyeballs in debt, I can see by the fact you have two new cars and a half-million-dollar home on the lake that money's not an issue. So it would probably be hard for you to understand."

No debt. Just good money management, disciplined spending habits, wise investing and savings. "Try me." He followed the road she pointed to, where the pet shop must be.

"I have a tough time accepting help and handouts because it reminds me too much of Mom having to scrounge for food, clothes and shelter after Dad left us destitute."

"Caleb mentioned your dad left you guys. I'm sorry, Bri."

"Why? You're not the woman who lured him away, then left him to rot in a nursing home alone. Never mind. End of subject."

They drove several blocks in silence. Ian tried

to forget her vanilla perfume infiltrating the car and concentrated on the quaint town's bright and cozy Christmas village-style decor.

Green wreaths with regal red bows adorned the lampposts that lined both sidewalks. A pristine army of iridescent angel figurines blew trumpets along the median on Eagle's Way, the main street running through the center of town.

Starlit decorations were tacked above every street sign. Strings of lights draped nearly every shop. Ian bet this was beautiful to drive through at night. He needed to bring Tia to see it.

"Still up for being my tour guide?" He eyed Bri's arm in a doctorly fashion. But he was really assessing her mood. At this point, her fidgeting gave the impression she was more embarrassed at her outburst than angry at him.

He bit back a smile when he realized she'd kept the change.

"Sure. We'll get Tia's fish on the way out of town. Go there." Bri indicated the far end of Eagle's Way. His car jostled over parts of it that were still cobblestoned, causing Bri to cradle her arm. He slowed.

She pointed to an eclectic-looking shop. A sleek purple building with black-light effects. "That's On the Edge. It's an art and florist shop, plus interior design. She's in competition with the woman across the street whose business is sewing, home decor and custom drapes." Bri pointed to the establishment named Fringe. He slowed the car, taking the town in.

"The women are archenemies and their brawls are just about the most excitement we have in town. The cops go there regularly, but I suspect it's mostly because the coffee shop next to Fringe has better donuts than Dee-Dee's Donuts beside the police station."

Ian chuckled. Mitch had been right to tell him this town was a perfect place to raise a child. Yet the number of closed shops concerned him. He knew the town's lifeblood could hinge on whether Bri's lodge reopened and thrived, and whether they were able to expand the trauma center and thus provide local jobs.

Next Bri indicated a brick-style brownstone turned into a storefront. "That's MeadowLark Laundry, owned by twin siblings, Meadow and Lark. They're two of the few people our age in town. But Meadow's away at college right now and Lark's in some kind of skip-tracer school. He's a P.I. on the side."

"Hey, that's my neighbor's shop." Ian indicated the LOLZ sign. Ellie told him she had an internet coffee shop catering to young people but he hadn't seen it yet. "She mentioned part of her business proceeds go toward cancer research and anti-text-and-drive ads."

"I remember the conversation you had with her about chemo when Tia wandered to her home. I hope Ellie's going to be okay."

"Me, too. She's raising a granddaughter named Mara." He cleared his throat. "She was in a tragic accident earlier this year while trying to save a classmate. Long story, but that's why Ellie moved here."

"Beside Fringe is Gulpie's Gas. Only station in town. Used to be called Not Your Mother's Guzzler. At the other end of town is EMS, police, city hall and the fire department. Lem's library is there, too. I'd like to take Tia once I can drive again."

"Tia loves to read. Much like you," Ian said.

She brushed a stray hair behind her ear and nodded ahead to the town square, really a circle. "You know Sully's, obviously, since we went there the other night."

He remembered. Unfortunately he also remembered the ache that gripped him to see Tia interacting with a mother figure.

"Next to that is Dulce Jo's Nook, a Victorian coffee shop and bookstore. Then, above the bank is an upscale restaurant called Golden Terrace."

He'd heard they had great dinner food. "Ever been there?"

"No, I haven't. Believe it or not, despite this being a small town, a world-class chef owns the place. It's upscale and pricey. Out of my budget, but I've heard the food's amazing."

Since she'd never eaten there, that's where he'd take her. Her stylish white skirt, vibrant red top and sparkly gunmetal boots would be fine at an upscale place.

Not that he cared what she wore, but she'd care. He didn't want her to feel underdressed or out of place. Of course, Bri could wear a potato sack and look classy. He chided himself for noticing her attractiveness. Hard not to, though. He refocused on the town and her tour. He'd missed the last thing she'd said.

"Most eateries are on the square. That brings the town together, because people get their food and sit out on patio furniture or mingle. Load'Em has great Chicago-style hot dogs. The owner also sells paintballs and airsoft ammo, so his shop name has duplicate meaning. He's new in town. I hear he's a hard-core war veteran. I don't doubt it, because he's even more dark and brooding than you."

Ouch. Ian stared at Bri. Didn't know whether to laugh or seethe. He decided to land somewhere in between. "News flash, Bri. Deployment didn't harden me. Divorce did," he snapped.

Bri eyed him nervously, then continued pointing out buildings. "Baldies is a barber shop. Ruffled Feathers is a kid-centric beauty salon. The business next to it is Reruns. They sell second-hand clothes and family-friendly DVD rentals. Run by a couple of friends. Back there's a drive-in."

"Wow. You don't see many of those nowadays. We'll have to take Tia sometime. Uh, I mean, I will."

She shrugged. "I'd tag along. I missed it a lot when I moved away. I'm glad I'm back, even though it took Mom's illness and death to bring me to my senses and back to my roots."

Ian figured she meant her ex-boyfriend. The one Caleb warned might try to harass Bri. Not gonna happen. Not on Ian's watch. He'd failed Caleb once. He wouldn't make the same mistake twice. Like getting married again. Not happening. Which is why he'd cringed inside when Bri agreed to go to the drive-in. The way people in this small town talked, they'd assume things about the two of them.

He didn't want things to ever seem too cozy. People could get hurt, including Tia. He'd simply invite Brock along.

After touring the main business part of town, then gorgeous residential antebellum architecture that survived the period, Ian eyed his watch. "I should check on Tia." He pulled over and texted Kate. She texted back that Tia was fine but they wouldn't be done shopping for a few more hours.

Ian filled Bri in, then resumed driving. "She said she tried texting you, but you didn't respond"

Bri's body jolted upward. "My phone! I left it at home. Not that anyone other than Caleb, Kate and Eric ever call it."

"He still harassing you? And yes, I know about it."

"Occasionally. But I can handle him."

He cut her a glance. "Yeah, but never hurts to have help."

"Except your and Caleb's idea of 'help' equates to pulverizing the guy."

Ian grinned. "Hey, whatever works. Seriously, tell me if he's bothering you. Or if his threats escalate. I mean it, Bri."

"I will. Eric doesn't know Caleb's deployed. Since he thinks Caleb's here with me, I'm sure he'll leave me alone."

"I'm not convinced. According to Caleb, he's a real creep."

"Which probably makes you wonder why I was stupid enough to date him. Or stay with him for a year."

Ian shrugged. "Hey, I have no stones to throw. I was a doctor with a drug-addicted wife and didn't even know it."

"Think that's why Ava and your marriage didn't last?"

He flinched "I don't know. Could've been the war. Or maybe it was just me."

"I'm not convinced," Bri said.

He shrugged off the fuzzy feelings as they went to the lawn-and-hardware store for small renovation supplies. Grabbed a few landscape items for Bri's place, though she protested. "People are more apt to rent places with attractive yards. Since you're turning your seven lakeside cabins into permanent rentals for income, it's prudent." He knew she'd planned to use the remaining retreat center cabins for seasonal and vacation campers and rentals.

She nodded but trod stiffly to another aisle. A whimsical winged garden gnome caught his eye. He snuck it into the cart and set his jacket over it. It would make a fitting Christmas gift from him and Tia. He picked out five large, festive outdoor wreaths for himself, Mitch, Lem, Bri and his neighbor Ellie.

He selected a monkey-faced planter for Kate and a tiny tractor replica for Lauren. He and Mitch were going in together on Fruit-of-the-Month Club gifts for their trauma center employees, but Ian grabbed a slew of culinary herb-and-spice seeds plus tiny pod planters, anyway, to add a personal touch.

He felt lame getting everyone garden stuff for Christmas, but time had gotten away from him.

They'd appreciate the gifts nonetheless. Everyone understood his current life chaos.

Yet it was far better than two months ago, thanks to Bri.

He eyed her from across the aisle, knowing that if he were a praying man, he'd say a heartfelt thank-you. The words wouldn't release from his mouth, though. Teeth clenched, Ian pressed on.

Excitement welled in Bri when she noticed Ian's cart piled high with wreaths, tinsel, bows, garland and bulbs. One package was vivid silver-sapphire bulbs, the other swirly gold scrolls on bright neon-pink. One stamped with the year was in the shape of a multitoned glitter fairy wearing a tiny purple organza tutu. "Aww! You're decorating with Tia, after all. Yay, Ian!"

"Yeah, even though tomorrow's Christmas Eve."

"Hey, better late than not at all."

"No decorations is part of Tia's rift with me. I can easily remedy that by picking up some lights and a tree, but confess I have no idea where I'm going wrong with those icky eggs." They laughed together.

The sound swept through and curled around her heart. Good to see Ian jovial. "I'll do some snooping. You're a good dad, Ian." She grew thoughtful. "You know, I think it would help if they were green."

"The lights?" They checked out and headed to the car.

"No. The eggs. Tia is very creative. Get her the Dr. Seuss book. Read it, then feed her some green eggs and ham."

Ian's face blanked for ten beats, then pinched. "In my line of work, green protein means people take unpleasant trips to my E.R."

She giggled. "You dye them, silly. I'll help."

Ian drove them to the grocery store to get ham, eggs and food coloring. Bri smiled when Ian slipped packages of Christmas cookie dough and a star-shaped cutter, decorative icing and colorful sprinkles in his cart. "For cookie trees?"

"Yeah. Although I don't want Tia to think I'm indulging her to gain her affection."

At the car, Ian put their purchased groceries into a battery-operated cooler. Bri then set into his roomy cooler the few staples she'd picked up, too. "Did you think to get ant killer?"

He straightened, scowling. "No, it's a known carcinogen that causes leukemia in children. Most exterminating chemicals are."

"I meant cinnamon. Ants don't like it so they stay away." Right now, she wished she could sprinkle a little on him. His curtness made her stomach drop.

His jaw clenched and he studied her under hooded eyes. Whether remorse or sulking, she didn't know.

His warm hand on her shoulder got her attention. "Sorry."

One word. Yet every emotion was packed into it. She couldn't turn. Couldn't look at his face right now. She'd burst out crying. For both of them.

Each wounded in their own way, like two raging animals lashing out at each other. The vivid image gave her the courage to look him in the eye.

"It would benefit us both if we'd stop snapping and snarling at each other, put our heads together and figure out how to get past it. Something's gotta give, Ian. Your brooding and my pouting. We can't go on like this. Tia will pick up on it."

A muscle rippled along his jaw. He studied her for a good ten seconds, then shut the car trunk. Firmly. Like the subject.

He pulled out his phone and dialed. "Hey, Kate, let's meet up for dinner at the Golden Terrace. I want Tia to see the lights downtown." Pause, then, "Why not? Where you at?" Ian scowled. "Fine. Meet me after dinner on the square." He clicked off and slid into the car. "I promised to take Tia to get a tree this evening.

She can see lights on the way, I guess. Kate can't meet for dinner."

Bri recalled him saying they were eating at the Golden Terrace. "I hope it's not an inconvenience to drive me home first."

He braked in the parking lot and looked at her. "Why? You haven't had dinner yet. I promised to feed you."

"Golden Terrace isn't my style. I'm more of a grab a BLT and sit out on the deck watching forest critters in the woods kind of girl." She didn't want to admit how low on cash she was.

"I'm buying. Mitch says they have great T-bone steaks. And rumor has it that's your favorite." Now his voice sounded teasing.

"If you're buying, I'm getting two steaks." She grinned.

Ian drove toward the middle of town. A screech, then a horrific crashing of glass and metal caused Bri's hand to grab the dash as Ian braked hard. "Oh, my word, someone just hit that guy on a bike!" Pieces of the motorcycle spun and bounced all over the road. "Oh, no, Ian!"

But by the time Bri's sentence ended, Ian had thrown open the door, and was sprinting to the scene of an accident that put ice in Bri's veins.

No way did someone not get seriously hurt in that. Breath short, she exited the car on trembling legs and rushed to where Ian and others crouched over the motorcycle rider. Several people were already on the phone.

"Sir, hold still," Ian directed the young man, who blinked awake, to Bri's relief. Sirens wailed in the distance now. Bri remembered how Ian being at her side calmed her. She closed her eyes and thanked God for having a doctor right here.

A doctor like Ian.

Paramedics loaded the man in, and Ian told them he'd meet them at the trauma center. "Mitch is gonna have a tough time with this one," Ian said as they followed the ambulance. "And so is Tia. I promised to take her to get a tree and see lights."

He looked so vulnerable, so torn, Bri couldn't keep her hand from clutching his forearm in a show of support. "She'll understand." *I hope.*

"I don't know. Tia's so vulnerable because of all her mother's broken promises. This could likely widen the chasm." His voice broke like the motorcycle. "I was gonna get you a tree, too."

"Oh, Ian, don't fret over me. I have a tree, in my bedroom. It's Caleb's. A four footer with key chains for ornaments. He's been collecting them since he was a kid. I keep it in my room because it makes me feel safer at night. Having his things and wearing his hoodies makes me feel close to him."

His forearm flexed under her hand, making

her aware of the muscles, and how able-bodied he'd been helping the young man, who'd stopped breathing shortly after Bri had knelt by him. No way could Ian not go to the trauma center. The man needed lifesaving surgery and Ian was the only anesthesiologist in town. "Sometimes I wish Caleb wouldn't share so much."

"With me?"

"No, about medical things. I don't know how you do it."

"And I don't know how you managed to wrangle a room full of romping preschoolers at the day care you owned. We all have gifts, Bri. It's whether people choose to use their gifts for good or not."

"Aha!" She aimed a finger at his cheek. "I knew it."

He cut a glance her way as he neared EPTC's lot. "What?"

"You do believe."

He shrugged, looking defensive at first. Then, surprisingly, his face softened. "What you said earlier about taming our reactions to one another made sense. But while it sounds good in theory, I don't have a solution."

"Praying helps." She braced for a harsh reaction. While annoyance flickered in his eyes, it wasn't the fireball she expected.

"I'll keep that in mind." He turned and hoofed

it to the trauma center ambulance bay, where
Mitch, Lauren and Kate met him. Tia stood wide-
eyed inside a window. Bri wiggled fingers at her
and went in to get her out of there. Lem stood
with her, but told Bri he needed to write a message for Lauren that he would wait with Tia at
Bri's.

Ian saw Kate, stood abruptly and whirled
around as if simultaneously remembering and
looking for something. He said something to
Kate, who pointed where Bri kept Tia distracted
from the gurney being wheeled quickly inside.

Ian saw that Tia was with Bri, and tangible relief washed over his face. He raised his gaze from
Tia to Bri, and their gazes connected through
the glass. Deep gratitude swam in his eyes as he
mouthed slowly, "Thank you."

Bri nodded. Put her hands to Tia's shoulders
to keep her facing the other way and tried her
best not to let the adoration in Ian's eyes get to
her. Adoration directed at Bri this time, and un-
quenchable love for Tia.

The way Bri had felt that moment their gazes
connected over the chaos drew her in a way that
made her realize she was growing to trust him—
more than she ever had with Eric.

"Ready?" She directed Lem to where Ian had
parked, his door still open. Bri laughed. Lem and
Tia loaded, Bri carefully drove one-armed to her

cabin at a snail's pace since she wasn't allowed to drive yet.

"You sure you're s'pose to be doing this?"

"What, driving?" Bri grinned and winked. "Sure."

Lem cast her and her sling a grandfatherly look and a grin that said he knew she absolutely was not supposed to be driving.

What harm could come? It was just across the parking lot.

And down one tiny road. And one itty corner.

Once at her place, Lem and Tia helped carry in and put away her groceries. Bri put Lem up to watching Tia while she unloaded gifts, drove to Ian's, lifted the key from his planter and unloaded his things. Longing swept through her when she got a good look at the huge wreaths. "So beautiful. Mama would have loved that on her lodge." A knot sat in Bri's throat because all of the Christmas decorations had mildewed in last spring's flood.

The river made Bri suddenly remember they'd forgotten the fish. "Could you watch her a few moments more?" she asked Lem once she was back at her cabin. He happily obliged while Bri snuck into the bedroom and used her landline to call the pet store, which would be closed before she had a chance to get back there tonight.

Please, be open on Christmas Eve.

Otherwise, Tia wouldn't get her Christmas fish.

"Sorry, no can do," the manager of the fish department told Bri on the phone. "We won't be open till the day after Christmas."

"What kind of pet store doesn't stay open on Christmas Eve?"

"The kind whose owner would rather spend time with his own family than make a ton of money."

"I see. I'm sorry then for sounding difficult."

"Sure. We'll hold the betta for you until after Christmas. I hope the little one has other gifts to tide her over."

Not a gift she'd really wanted. Bri ended the call with her hopes diving for Ian and Tia to have a good Christmas. But, at least they had each other. If only Tia could realize how hard Ian was trying, and that he couldn't help having to work sometimes.

Bri's stomach growled on the way back to the playroom, reminding her they hadn't eaten. Oh, well, probably for the best. The last thing she wanted to endure was an awkward dinner conversation with Tia's brooding dad.

Paused at the playroom door watching Tia, enthralled as Lem read a Bible storybook to her, Bri hoped Ian would take her advice and truly consider that talking to God about all his troubles could make a huge difference.

Chapter Five

What would make the difference? Ian wondered at 5:00 a.m. Christmas Eve morning when he went to Bri's to pick up Tia, who glared at him from the playroom door. "You ruined everything!"

He knelt on Bri's woodland tapestry rug. "Tia, you got to help Miss Bri decorate her home last night. She said Lem even showed you how to make homemade ornaments before he left. They look wonderful." He beamed at the colorful construction paper rings draped on Bri's molding and the paper-and-glitter snowflakes on her walls and tree. "We have decorations to put up at our house, too. That's why I'm here so early to get you."

"You're not early. You're very late. We waited a long time and you never came back." Her voice cracked, and her chin trembled. Stark fear and vulnerability flushed the anger from her face.

She put her face down, composure crumpled, shoulders quaked.

In that instant Ian realized she had been afraid he'd left for good. As she was starting to figure out Ava had done. "I'd never leave you, Tia." He reached for her.

She jerked her shoulder from his grasp and quivered to keep her sobs in. Bri stood in the doorway with worried, caring eyes.

Ian leaned in. "Tia, I'm sorry our plans went awry. The man who hit the motorcycle had fallen ill while driving. I had to take care of him, too." His aneurysm had required a long, delicate surgery. Then the motorcycle victim coded. Twice. Following that, a tragic trampoline accident had paralyzed a man, who'd purchased it for his child's Christmas present.

Yet Ian wouldn't dare say all that to Tia.

His phone rang. It was his mother, probably wondering what time he planned on leaving Lem's to drive to her home this evening, so she could see Tia open her presents Christmas morning. He'd call her back in a bit. For now, he wanted to decorate.

"Hey, Tia, I have a surprise waiting for you at home."

She squealed and clapped. "A puppy?"

His spirits took a nosedive. "No, but I think you'll like it, anyway."

Her face lit with tentative hope. "A fishy?"

Ugh. Strike two.

"Let's head over and see."

She approached with an expressionless face. Clearly, she expected to be further disappointed. Hadn't life proved it to be so? Ian motioned Bri to follow. She helped Tia on with her coat, and the trio walked over to his place to decorate. Hopefully, it would cheer Tia up to see the tree. By the time Ian dug it out of the box, his mom called twice more. Jenny Shupe wasn't one to phone others obsessively. Maybe something was wrong. He called back. "Hey, Mom. Everything okay?" If life threw one more curveball at him...

"Everything's fine. Sorry to worry you." Relief hit. She sounded chipper. Voices invaded the background. "Oh!" she said excitedly. "Your siblings just arrived. Let me call you back."

"Sure." Ian used the time to put the tree together.

Tia wandered into the family room and gasped. Her eyes brightened and a grin tugged her mouth up, though she tried to hide it when Ian saw. Bri moved next to him. Her arm brushed his in what he instinctually knew was a show of solidarity.

He leaned to Bri, and whispered, "Tia's smile sorely tempts me to be a one-time burglar. Break into Pawsome Pets, nab a particular betta so she'll have Jonah in time for Christmas."

Bri smiled. "I can see the headlines now. *'One of Eagle Point's most respectable doctors shocked the community today in an arrest for stealing a dollar-sixty-five fish....'*"

He grinned. Kept the skin of his arm next to hers simply because it had been a long time since he'd felt anything that sweet. He wished he could express to her how much it meant. He wanted to bottle the feeling and keep it.

Tia began avidly investigating the tree and tinsel. She tossed its iridescent white-on-silver strands over her shoulders like a cape and began circling the tree, arms flapping like a nativity angel. Bri's giggle mingled with Ian's chuckle.

Ian leaned close to Bri again and kept low tones. "To my credit, the fishbowl and food cost seven bucks. Technically still a misdemeanor." Ian grinned. He looked at Bri and reveled in not only how pretty her eyes were close up, but just how huge a part she played in reviving joy for him and Tia. Just by being herself. Like now. Her cheeks tinged pink at his open perusal, so he put some space between them.

Tia rushed up, took Bri's hand and jumped up and down. "It's a tree! A tree! A tree!"

Bri pretended surprise. "A tree! How exciting!" She winked at Ian above Tia's head. It did funny stuff to his heart.

None of those other fuzzy feelings, though.

Not even if she did look breathtaking in a sapphire-blue frock that dazzled like Eagle Point Lake at sunrise. Silver dangly earrings brushed her jawbone at the juncture of an elegant neck. Ian tore his gaze and set his focus where it should be: on his daughter.

He set about opening other boxes of decorations and refocused on Tia. She didn't seem perturbed that he'd gotten the tree without her. Thankfully, the Christmas-tree-farm owner had sold him a tree at four this morning after he'd left the trauma center.

Ian handed Tia her own special ornament. She gasped and hugged the fairy to her heart, then moved toward him like a flash but stopped. "Thank you," she said in a small voice.

Oh, how he wished she'd gone ahead with the hug. His phone rang again. "Hey, Mom."

"Hi, son." His mom's telltale hesitation made him pace. "Listen, we need to change plans up for Christmas. Your dad just surprised me with Mississippi Christmas riverboat cruise tickets. I realize I invited you kids over for Christmas Day and the day after Christmas, but the boat leaves this evening. Would it be a hardship to have our family Christmas meal for lunch today instead of dinner tomorrow?"

Ian thought of Lem. He might be disappointed, but he'd understand. Lem had Mitch, Lauren and others coming. Ian told his mom he'd call her back, then dialed Lem, who was gracious about Ian's cancellation. "Just so long as you and little T start coming to my Saturday chili cook-offs," he'd said. Then told Ian he knew he didn't get to see his parents and siblings together often these days. Ian hung up, knowing Lem was right and that his life needed a serious breather. But he'd taken on all these cabin renovations....

Of course, in return he had dependable child care, which eased his stress. Ian called his mom back. "That would be fine."

"Good, then I'll let you go so you can get things ready." Ian ended the call with his to-do list proliferating in his head. He eyed his watch. Two-hour drive to St. Louis. He still needed to decorate his house, wrap presents and pack a bag for himself and Tia.

Another thought erupted. What about Bri? She might not feel comfortable going to Lem's by herself now that Kate couldn't be there. Kate had offered last night to take the Christmas Eve night shift so a single mother R.N. could spend Christmas Eve and Christmas morning with her children.

Plus Tia had been super-excited to learn Bri would be with them on Christmas Eve day. What to do?

He observed Bri, smiling at Tia, while seated

on his love seat. He was stricken by how its color seemed more lively dove than doom-cloud gray with her on it. No surprise. Bri's demeanor tended to brighten all she came in contact with. Well, with the exception of ladders, of course.

Ian held up boxes. "Who wants to help decorate?"

Tia erupted in squeals, and the trio decorated in frenzied laughter with festive music playing in the background.

Ian realized he had joined their laughter at some point. He'd also gotten that cozy, homey family feeling. Not good. Not at all.

But there was no way he could leave Bri home alone on Christmas. Not only did the thought sadden him, Caleb would be hurt, as well. Ian couldn't assume she'd go to Lem's. He was afraid she'd isolate herself if he simply excused himself and Tia from going to Lem's. He sighed. Knew what he needed to do.

That didn't make it easy. She'd probably assume he'd only invited her because he felt sorry for her and refuse to go because of her issue with hating to feel like someone's charity case. He found her feeding Tia breakfast. She'd made herself at home in his kitchen. The sight of her with his apron on stirred equal shock, awe and anger. She tensed, so she'd caught whiffs of his ill feelings about a woman making herself at home in his life. Doubtful she'd go, but he was obligated to ask. "Bri, we've had a change in plans at my folks' house. They want us to actually come today."

She blinked. "I thought you were going to Lem's?"

"I was, but I just called and canceled." He explained about the riverboat thing.

"I understand. It's not a problem. I've got plenty to do here and stuff to keep me occupied."

"In other words, you won't go to Lem's."

She shrugged. Busied herself doing tasks in his kitchen. He wished she'd take his apron off.

He scratched his jaw. "Actually, I'm inviting you along."

Tia squealed. "Yay! Grandma will love you!"

Bri blinked at Tia, then narrowed her gaze at Ian as if to protest the fact that he'd asked her in front of Tia, which gave her less of an out. Hands on her hips, she said, "I'd be delighted to accompany the two of you."

This wasn't so bad.

Bri's shoulders relaxed twenty minutes into arriving at Ian's parents' home in an affluent St. Louis suburb. "Your dad really knows how to tickle those ivories." Bri smiled as Ian's brothers and sister gathered around the piano, while Ian's dad's fingers danced over its keys in a rendition of "Jingle Bell Rock."

"Come on, Ian! Join us." His mom, Jenny, waved him over.

Ian's ears tinged. He darted a glance at Bri. "No, thanks."

Bri bit her lip to keep from smiling that he was nervous to sing in front of her. Tia inched forward. Her grandpa nodded at her, then the lyric booklet. She tried her best to sing along.

The Shupe family smiling and singing together brought joy to Bri's heart, as did the tender way Ian watched Tia interact with the family her mother had kept her from.

Another sort of knot settled in Bri's throat and made her nose burn. "Excuse me," she said. "Allergies," she explained to Ian's mom. Then walked as calmly to the great room as she could, leaned against the window and let the tears roll.

The floor creaked behind her. She made a play of digging for her allergy medication and dabbing her nose with the wadded tissue, even though her allergies weren't really the problem.

"Hey, you okay?" Voice like velvet. Deep. Rich. Soothing. And as caring as the day he'd said those very words on the asphalt after she'd taken a tumble off the ladder.

Because she didn't trust her mouth to speak, she nodded. He came around to peer at her face.

Bri tried to look away, especially since the deep concern and gentle care in his eyes made it harder for her to dam the emotions pressing for release.

"Allergies," she managed to croak out.

She felt his silent gaze on her for a few moments, then he said, "Yeah. They bothered me, too, especially after my divorce."

She peered up. His eyes roved over her face and he looked as if he was about to pull her in for a hug. If he did, the dam would collapse for sure. "Excuse me," she said and stepped out from his overpowering presence that threatened to pulverize every wall she'd spent the past six months building.

When she'd composed herself, Ian's mom was in the hallway getting linens out. "Are you feeling all right, dear? I can show you to your room if you'd like to take a nap before lunch?"

Bri smiled. She liked Ian's mom. A lot. Even as she ached for her own. "Thank you, but I'm feeling a bit better."

"Well, you just let me know if you change your mind. You hafta make yourself at home here." She smiled kindly. Ian walked up behind her, seeking to catch and hold Bri's gaze. She could barely make eye contact. "Ian, show her around."

He nodded. When Ian's mom went to the other room, Bri smiled despite her melancholy over missing her own mom. "Your mom's like a breeze of fresh air."

Ian laughed. "Or like a hurricane, depending on whether she wants her way over something."

Bri followed where he motioned onto the side deck. "She's also a dead ringer for Paula Deen."

"She cooks as well, too." Ian led Bri down to a brick patio with white wrought-iron seating near trees that were probably here before the house. "So," he said. "This is the yard." He waved at the grass, pond and walk.

Bri laughed. "Really? I never would have guessed."

He shrugged. "Hey, I never claimed to be as good a tour guide as you." He motioned to the side yard. "This way. You have to meet Homer the goat."

"A goat?" Bri said a few seconds later. "Does he bite?"

Ian laughed loudly. "No. But if he doesn't like you, he'll run and head butt you. He might look old and decrepit, but believe me, he's strong."

"What does he do if he likes you?"

"Probably try to chew that white-silk hair of yours." His gaze snagged on it, causing the air to tense around them.

Bri petted Homer, who aggressively trailed her across the yard, up the steps and to the door. Bri looked to Ian. "Help?"

He shook his head. "Looks like he's taken a shine to you."

For a brief instant, the way Ian looked at her, it almost seemed like he could, too.

Bri tried to wave her hands at Homer. "Shoo. Go on, now."

Homer only bleated at her. And Ian chuckled. "He wants in."

"Your mother lets a goat in the house?"

Ian took the steps two at a time, reminding her just how agile and athletic he was. "No, he has a play yard." He opened a little gate and Homer dashed in.

Back inside, the family waved Ian and Bri over. They avidly protested until Tia turned puppy eyes up to her dad and said, "Please sing with us?" She eyed Bri also. "You, too?"

Bri groaned inwardly. She'd do it for Tia. Ian's dad went to town on the piano again, singing "Carol of the Bells," then a chipmunk song, which Tia giggled through more than sang.

While Bri didn't have the greatest singing voice, she found herself bouncing and singing along. Ian smiled beside her.

After a delicious lunch, Ian's mom announced, "Time for the gift exchange. Everyone gather 'round the tree."

Bri went with the family, feeling less adrift

than a day ago. She was glad she hadn't let pride keep her away from this special time. Plus, she'd get to see Tia open her gifts.

After Ian and his two brothers carried gifts in, everyone settled around in a circle on the floor. Ian sat next to Bri, and Tia settled halfway on her grandma's lap and halfway on her aunt's lap. Ian's sister, Leah, darted curious glances Bri's way. When Ian caught on to it, he scooted a bit, putting a few more inches of space between himself and Bri. Fine with her. She didn't want anyone getting the wrong idea, either.

Ian's dad donned a fuzzy reindeer hat whose antlers blinked colorful lights that made Tia giggle. He pulled out a smaller pair and put it on her head, then started passing out presents.

Surprise overtook Bri when he set a gift in her lap. "That's from me and Ian's mom."

"Oh, but I didn't get you anything!" She tried to push the present back, so Ian pushed her hand down.

Ian's dad chuckled and said, "He told us you'd try to do that." He grew serious. "You're gifting our family with the peace of knowing that Tia's in good hands while Ian works. Nothing beats the gift of your presence, Bri. That's a little token from the family to show how much you're appreciated."

She blinked swiftly, hating that all eyes were on her, waiting expectantly for her to open it. She peeled the tape delicately while anticipation electrified the air.

"Ian's siblings went in on it," Ian's mom said.

The paper was so gorgeous, Bri didn't want to destroy it. But in a flash of impatience, Tia trundled over in her vivid yellow tutu and plopped on her knees in front of Bri. "You do it like this." With one motion, Tia dug fingers into the paper and ripped it to shreds. The room erupted in laughter, including Bri. "Well, I'm glad the expert helped me out."

"Open it!" Tia clapped, excitedly. Ian eyed her carefully.

Bri slid open the box and pulled out a gorgeous Tiffany glass wall hanging that contained an eagle flying amid a sunset. "It's beautiful," Bri breathed, then lifted it to find a pretty quilted tapestry in her cabin's colors.

Bri was still smiling when Ian shoved another gift at her.

"Well, son! That's no way to treat your lady friend."

Ian's jaw clenched for some reason. Why? Could it be because his mom and sister kept referring to Bri as Ian's "lady friend" rather than the babysitter, despite Ian compulsively correcting them?

Ian nodded to her gift. "You gonna open it?"

Bri peeled back the paper to find the cutest little garden gnome ever. Ian got up and reached behind the chair. Pulled out a wreath. One she'd had her eye on. "I know Christmastime is almost over, but this would look nice on your lodge year-round."

She took the beautiful wreath and met Ian's gaze. "Thank you." If she didn't think it would both make him freak out and fuel his mom and sister's matchmaking, Bri would hug him. "This means a lot, Ian."

"It means a lot that you're in our lives."

Not used to that kind of sentimentality from her typically brooding doctor, Bri nodded and sat back down, trying to convince herself the little flips in her tummy were from eating too much of Ian's mom's Christmas fudge. As they ate, a text came in to Ian's phone from Ava that caused him to scowl. Bri averted her eyes.

After the family exchanged gifts, lively laughter and hugs, Ian's sister approached Bri. "Would you mind helping me clean the kitchen up, so she can pack and leave early for her trip?"

Bri smiled and stood. "Not at all."

Ian didn't like the looks of this. His sister was worse than Kate in terms of matchmaking. He didn't like her luring Bri away when his mom had a perfectly good dishwasher.

Tia's grandpa and uncles took her to see Homer the goat, which gave Ian a chance to text Ava back. She lived in St. Louis yet declined to see Tia. Tia would be devastated. He looked up on someone's approach. "Hey, Mom."

Ian's mom pulled him into the pantry. "What's going on?"

He shrugged. "Ava's being her typical self."

She shook her head sadly. "So she's not even willing to meet us if we drive Tia there?"

"Afraid not. She demanded I stop texting her or she'll change her number, call the cops and sue me for harassment. She won't even get Tia a card. I offered to buy one on her behalf."

"Ian, at some point you have to stop covering. Tia has to know Ava's the issue and not you. Tia resents you enough as it is."

"I know. But I can't in good conscience give her mom a bad rap in Tia's eyes."

"Ava does a fine job of that herself. You need to move on and find yourself a decent wife. One who'd be a loving mother to little T." His mom scurried over and peeked through the crack in the doorway leading to the kitchen. "So, Bri—"

"Is nothing but our babysitter, Mom."

"Uh-huh. Well, the minute it becomes more, you let me know."

Ian gritted his teeth, patience leaking like helium from a punctured balloon. "It *won't* become more. Stop meddling."

She blinked big, wide eyes, trying to look innocent.

"You're worse than Leah," he said. He needed to declare war on his mom and sister's matchmaking efforts. Bring in the big guns. Something to deter and thwart them.

He didn't have the time, or the heart, for this nonsense.

His mom stopped observing Bri and brought Ian a yellow-and-green festive envelope. "Son, I need another favor. I promised Tia a Make-A-Zoo trip near our home. It's a stuffed animal factory where kids make the animals. She had her heart set on it and has never been. That was our gift to her but the certificate can only be used tonight on Christmas Eve. We'll be on the Mississippi. Would you take Tia for me?"

"I can do that. You and Dad have a good time." Ian schooled his outer reaction but gritted his proverbial inner teeth, knowing he had a serious dilemma. His siblings were flying out early morning the day after Christmas.

He didn't fancy the notion of just Bri, him and Tia somewhere alone for an extended period during the holiday season. Too many people would comment about what a cute family they were.

He needed a solution ASAP. He went outside. Paced the yard.

Tia stood with his family and Bri in the courtyard below. Tia brushed a hand along the tree's piney branches and smooth needles. "At least this ol' tree has its pj's on."

PJ! That's it. Ian would hit Brock up to go. Hadn't Brock mentioned not going home for Christmas? Not only that, Brock had been checking Bri out the day they'd met at the lodge. This could totally work in his favor and counteract his family's matchmaking.

Ian dialed Brock's number, but got his voice mail.

Brock phoned back. "Hey, dude. Whut-up?"

"Hey, Brock. I need another favor. Can you meet me in St. Louis this evening?"

"Probably. Everything okay?" His rescuer voice kicked in.

"Yeah. I need you to come endure an M.A.Z. with me."

"What's M.A.Z.? Sounds like a covert military operation."

Ian burst out laughing. "Well, it sort of is. M.A.Z. is Make-A-Zoo where kids craft soft toys themselves."

Four seconds of total silence. "Dude, seriously? You want me to go to a stuffed-animal factory with you? For real?"

"C'mon, you owe me for all the training you get at EPTC."

"Yeah, but pastel fluffy things? Come on. That's asking a lot. If my teammates found out, I'd never hear the end. Besides, don't you think that would be a great time for you and T to bond?"

"Well, it *would,* except that she can't stand to be around me, number one, and two, Bri's here, too."

"Bri, the tall blonde who owns the lodge?"

"Yep."

"*Dude,* I'm *totally* there."

Four hours later, Brock shoved a piece of plush, fuzzy material at Ian's chest at their next Make-A-Zoo station. "Dude, I don't care how big, bad, macho and brave you are. When a kid hands you an empty cloth animal carcass, you stuff it."

Ian laughed and took the floppy squirrel Tia picked out.

"What are you making?" Ian asked Bri, standing nearby with hers.

"A monkey for Kate and a Cardinals frog for Caleb with a sentimental recorded message inside." Her voice caught on her brother's name, reminding Ian that Bri had no one for Christmas. He suddenly felt like a heel for being so paranoid about his family matchmaking. Besides, his plan had backfired, anyway, he thought while watching Brock flirt with his sister, Leah.

He'd have to come up with a new battle plan. A stronger defense against the emotions he was beginning to feel every time he witnessed Bri interact with his daughter.

Chapter Six

"That was a blast, Ian. Thank you," Bri said on the two-hour drive back to Eagle Point on Christmas Day the following morning. "I'm glad your parents were able to see Tia open all her gifts before they left on Christmas Eve. It was nice of them to put us all up for the night."

He nodded. But had grown solemn. In fact, he had been since Brock ended up driving his sister to the airport this morning.

"Everything okay, Ian? You seem—"

"Fine."

Bri settled deeper in the car cushions, wishing she'd sat in the back with Tia, asleep in her booster seat.

Bri tilted her seat back and closed her eyes to rest.

"We're here." Ian's robust hand shook her shoulder. Tia blinked awake in the back. Bri rubbed her eyes and realized they were at her cabin. A strange sense of disappointment hit that their time would be over, despite Ian's bad mood. Bri exited the car. At least she hadn't had to spend all of Christmas alone.

She leaned in and hugged Tia. "Merry Christmas, little fairy elf." She pinched Tia's cheek.

Tia giggled and wiggled her head to tinkle her antlers. "I'm not a fairy elf, silly. I'm a fairy reindeer."

"I see." Bri went to grab her suitcase, but Ian beat her to it. He hadn't said two sentences since stopping the car. With him in that kind of mood, she was better off alone at her cabin.

He wheeled her suitcase inside and carried her gifts in. He checked inside Bri's cabin to be sure everything was okay, then eyed Tia through the doorway.

"Merry Christmas, Ian."

He raised his chin, jaw hard. Eyes glinted, then softened some. "You, too. I hope my family didn't overwhelm you too much."

His statement socked her in the gut and brought tears to the back of her eyes. What on earth? She didn't typically cry. "I'd take overwhelming over absent and gone any day."

The way his face flickered let her know that might've come out harsh. "There's no need to apologize for your family. You should be glad they're all still here." She turned to go inside.

"You should go see him, Bri."

She whirled. "Who? My dad? Absolutely not. And I'd appreciate you not telling Caleb he needs to go see him, either."

"Caleb's the one who told me you need to go."

Her stomach burned like hot embers. "He's been to see him?"

Ian drew a breath, looking as if he was gauging how much to tell her. "That's something for you to discuss with your brother."

"Apparently my brother has no interest in talking to me about it, otherwise I wouldn't know less than you." She shook her head. "This conversation is dismised. If you'll excuse me—" She tried to shut the door, but his palm prevented it.

"I wasn't finished."

"Oh, yes, you were." She thought about shutting his fingers in the door. How could Caleb confide in Ian more than her? It stung. So did Caleb's betrayal of their pact not to forget what their dad had done. Of course, they'd made the pact when she was fifteen and he was fourteen, but still.

Ian removed his hand off the door. "We'll be back after I check on things at my place. Unless you'd rather go over there?"

"Huh?"

"I don't plan to leave you alone on Christmas, Bri."

That made her feel demoralized. "I'm fine." She didn't want to be someone's obligation. She wanted to be someone's choice. "Thanks for the lovely time with your family, Ian. Goodbye."

He stuffed hands in his pockets. "Suit yourself." He backed away, then shrugged and turned to go.

She shut the door and leaned against it. Stared at her golden walls but felt anything but happy. Gloomy was more like it. Her bird clock screeched. She jumped. Thought about tossing her shoe at it. Decided not to, knowing why she'd regret it.

Bri walked through the dim stillness of the room to the mantel and soaked in the smiling faces of nostalgia framed in wood and memories. "Oh, baby brother, how I miss you. Please stay safe," Bri whispered while brushing fingers over images of Caleb. Then her mother. "I miss you so much."

Bri suddenly felt so overwhelmed by a dark loneliness that she could barely breathe. What if something happened to Caleb? Then she'd certainly be all alone.

Except there was Ian. No wonder Caleb had asked him to watch over her. He knew how much more dangerous this deployment was going to be. It dawned on her that, for all she knew, Caleb's asking Ian to watch over her might've extend to "if I don't make it home…."

The thought dropped her to her knees. "Lord, please bring him home safely. And, as much as I hate to admit, he was right to have someone look out for me. Thank You for Ian. And for giving me a new family in the friendship of Kate, Lauren, Mitch and our church home." Even on Ian's grumpiest days, she'd take his presence over this terrible feeling of utter aloneness. She pulled a puzzle box down and sank to her rug with a farm scene.

A knock drew Bri off the rug and to the door.

Ian had returned…with Tia…and an armful of gifts.

Bri let them in, smiling at Tia, yet avoiding Ian's eyes. Guilt assailed her over her inability to admit she wanted—needed—not to be by herself today, and the cowardice that prevented her from looking him in the eyes and saying thank-you. Seems she'd let Eric's constant stream of harsh put-downs erode her confidence.

Tia stepped around Bri's puzzle in progress. She pushed a crookedly wrapped, heavily taped gift with tendrils of disheveled ribbon toward Bri and grinned. "I did that myself!"

"Wow. It looks like the job of a professional.

Good job!" Bri pretended not to notice unwrapped corners poking through.

"Come have a seat and I'll unwrap it." Bri ruffled Tia's hair. It smelled of strawberries, a scent that more and more was bringing out Bri's maternal instincts. In short, she was getting attached. She realized she wanted to keep them here. Truth was, she didn't want to be alone. She took her time putting on Christmas music, then served them hot cocoa.

Tia ignored the cocoa and pointed at the present. "You hafta open it!" Her face beamed excitedly as Bri sat.

Ian seated himself in the chair catty-corner to Bri's love seat, his knee almost touching hers. Because Tia stood between Bri's knees, there was nothing Bri could do about the contact. She flicked a gaze at Ian. He either didn't notice or didn't mind. She eyed the gifts he clutched in his lap but didn't ask. Bri began the arduous task of peeling layers of tape.

"Here, let me help you." Tia scratched holes in the paper.

Bri lifted up a miniature squirrel like the one she'd made at the stuffed toy store. Identical, in fact, except the small one wore a tiny purple tutu. "That's me!" Tia pushed the squirrel close to Bri, then indicated Bri's squirrel, poking out of her bag. "And that's you!" Tia set the bigger squirrel on Bri's lap, then cuddled the smaller squirrel in its paws.

Tears pricked her eyes. Then horror as Tia snatched a third animal from her coat and squished it beside the other two. "And that's my dad."

Ian's face paled. Bri coughed down her sip of cocoa. Ian didn't look as though he knew what to say at the moment. Bri knew the feeling. Ian bent forward, plucked the stuffed frog up. "Tia, where did you get this?"

"I sneaked it out of your suitcase, of course."

She reached for it. Ian lifted it up. Clearly, no way did he want her putting them together as a family.

Ian rose, presumably to take his empty cocoa cup into the kitchen. Bri held Tia's shoulders. "T, you realize I'm just the babysitter, right?"

Tia's face fell. Her chin fell against her chest, her gaze to the floor. Then she lifted soulful eyes so filled with hurt it gripped Bri's heart. "I wanted my mom for Christmas."

What should Bri say? She'd picked up that Ava had refused to come see Tia. But what had Ian told her? Bri needed to be careful. She hugged Tia close. "I'm so sorry. I know that had to be disappointing."

Tia snaked her arms around Bri's waist and held. Bri felt tears soak her shoulder. Ian came back in, paused in the doorway, eyes acutely watching. Bri tried to send a reassuring smile, but his expression remained stone faced. He should know Bri wouldn't say anything derogatory about Ava.

A pounding at the door, then someone running, then a whimper. What on earth? Bri practically vaulted over Tia to get to the door, but Ian beat her to it. He swung it open and scowled. At Bri.

"What? What is it?" Bri leaned out the doorway, past Ian's visible seething. His jaw clenched and his eyes were fierce with anger. Bri looked down. Inside a wicker basket with a big red bow sat a yellow Lab puppy who hadn't grown into his feet yet.

Bri dropped to her knees. "Oh!" She eyed Ian. "Did you?"

Puzzlement flickered across his face. He shook his head. "But something tells me *you* did."

She surged to her feet. "I certainly did not!"

Tia scrambled past Ian in the doorway. He tried to stop her, but she saw the dog, who instantly wagged his tail and tried to climb from the basket, but because he was so small, tottered back. "Oh! A puppy!" Tia grabbed Bri in a hug, but Bri held herself back. "Tia, it's not from me." Tia whirled and slammed her dad with a hug. "Thank you, thank you, thank you! I prayed and it came true! A puppy for Christmas!"

Ian's mouth fell open. Clamped shut. His arms came around to pat Tia. The puppy whimpered. "He's cold," Bri pointed out. She ignored Ian's caustic look as she lifted the basket and carried it inside. If he didn't want the dog, she'd keep it. Tia could play with it while she was here. Bri brought in what looked to be a month's supply of puppy food in a gift bag near his basket.

Ian shut the door with his foot and walked over to the couch, where Tia rushed as Bri set the basket down. The puppy whimpered and whined. Bri picked him up and held him close. Tia reached for him. The pup's tail wagged and he tried to scramble from Bri's arms to Tia's petting fingers.

"Here, sit back." Bri helped Tia situate with two elbows on throw pillows, then settled the puppy in her arms, feeling the heat of Ian's anger boring into her back. Tia snuggled the pup, who was too excited to sit. He tottered up on wobbly legs, put his paws to Tia's chest and licked her chin, eliciting giggles.

"I love him. I love him so much." She squeezed the dog. Maybe a little too tight, because the dog looked at Bri with eyes a little wider than before. "Here, not so hard. Be very gentle. He's obviously a baby."

Ian pulled papers out of a basket. A note. He stood, took it to the kitchen. "Tia, can you be very careful with the dog?"

"His name is Mistletoe," she informed Bri.

"Oh, is that right?"

"Yes. Because he came on Christmas and gave me kisses."

Bri nodded. "That sounds like a fine name. I'm going to get him some water. I'll be right back."

"I'm surprised you have the guts to come in here and face me," Ian bit out the second she walked to her utility room, since Tia could see them in the kitchen. His eyes had turned to blue ice.

Bri's jaw clenched. "I. Did. Not. Get. That. Dog."

"Then who did?"

"Beats me." She rummaged for a tiny bowl.

Ian's hand snaked out and grabbed her wrist. "Do *not* feed that dog."

"He might be thirsty."

"You feed or water him, and he's going to want to stay."

"You're not keeping him?"

"Absolutely not. Tia will just have to understand."

"Will she, Ian? Or is it you who lacks understanding?" Bri shoved past him. His hand on her shoulder blocked her.

"I'm not kidding, Bri. We cannot keep the dog."

"Then can I?"

Surprise flashed over his face and it was his turn to shove away.

Bri closed her eyes, and thought of something Tia said. She caught Ian's shirttail and dragged him backward. Annoyance flickered across his face. "Wait, Ian. She said she prayed for the dog."

Recall flickered in his eyes. "That didn't give you the right to go behind my back and arrange this."

Bri felt rage rising. "You have no right to assume I'm lying to you. Someone else got the dog, but maybe God put it in someone's heart to do so, knowing how Tia is struggling."

"A dog can't replace a parent."

"I know that. I had four stray dogs, plus a stray cat who slapped the living daylights out of them on a weekly basis."

He calmed down. "You're telling the truth?"

"Yes. I had no part in getting the dog."

He still didn't look as though he believed her, which irritated her. He had no reason not to trust her.

Other than he'd been married to a lying, cheating wife.

Bri calmed herself. "The fact of the matter is, Tia thinks God sent the dog."

"So, what? You have to cover for God now, because He didn't hear? Make her think He answered when in fact He didn't?"

"Maybe He did. She prayed for a dog. A yellow dog. It showed up on Christmas, like she asked. Who else knew about it?"

Bri had a point. Ian's insides still shook with anger. He racked his brain to think of who else Tia might've told she wanted a yellow dog for Christmas. He couldn't think of anyone who'd do something so over-the-top. That left Bri.

He dangled papers in his hand. "Obviously someone planned this. The dog is a rescue from the pound. He's had his shots, and here's a certificate for two years' worth of veterinary bills paid, plus a huge gift card for more food at Pawsome Pets."

"He's going to be a huge dog."

He sent her a wry look. "This is far from funny."

Bri snickered, anyway. "I'm sorry, Ian. I'm… happy for Tia."

"She *can't* keep the dog."

"Then let me keep Mistletoe here for her. I'll assume one hundred percent of the care and responsibility. Ian, please."

"Mistletoe?" He shifted. "She's already named it."

Not a question. A resignation. But for what? To keep the dog or get rid of it? He had no clue what to do. Because the truth was, he knew how painful it was to feel let down by God. The last thing he wanted Tia to feel was forgotten and overlooked by the one supreme being who supposedly epitomized love. It dawned on Ian who might've gotten the dog. "Kate."

Bri shook her head. "That blue Mazda wasn't her car."

Ian groaned. "Ellie. Well, it's not like I can yell at a lady undergoing chemo."

"Oh, dear." To Bri's credit, she looked as though she understood his dilemma. But he wasn't totally convinced of her innocence, either. Dogs just didn't appear on people's doorsteps. Especially not from a cancer-ridden woman fighting for her life.

On the other hand, Ellie most likely had cognitive impairment from her cancer treatments, which might explain her not getting his permission. Last thing he wanted to do was hurt Ellie. She had enough on her plate. Of course, so did he. And now there was one more demand on his time. A four-legged one with puppy breath and wrinkly jowls.

He sighed. "Fine. She can keep the dog."

Bri squealed and hugged him. It threw him for a loop. Electricity arced between them. Bri felt it, too, because she scrambled back, wide eyed. Scowled as if he was the cause of it.

"I'll need your help taking care of him."

"I told you I would. I meant it."

He shook his head. "I cannot believe someone did this." He waved Bri in. "I have something for you."

She followed. Tia snuggled with the playful
dog, who nipped and yipped at her wiggling fingertips amid squeals and giggles.

Ian handed Bri her gift. "That's from me."

She tore into it the way Tia would, causing Ian
to want to grin.

She gasped. It was the first season of her favorite TV show. "Wherever did you find this?"
She looked as happy with the Blu-ray boxed set
as Tia was with the dog. Her face fell. "But I don't
have a high-def-T.V."

Now Ian did grin. He loved being generous.
"Be right back." Bri watched him with curious
eyes as he went to his car and brought back a new
high-def television.

She gasped. "Oh, my word. You didn't!"

"I know you'll have a hard time accepting this,
but it was on sale, and your TV is ancient."

"Yes, it's on its last leg. You'll help me set it
up and show me how it works?"

He nodded. "Of course. We can do it today."
He pulled another gift out. "That's from Caleb."

Tears flooded her eyes. "How—?"

Ian smiled. "The day he called and I went to the

porch so you couldn't hear. He asked me to pick this up for you. It's what he wanted you to have."

She tore open the paper, blinking tears. She pulled a beautiful burgundy frame with an image of herself and Caleb. "I remember this," she breathed. "The day he left for deployment. He'd turned his phone and snapped a digital image of us." She smiled through a sheen of tears. Then peeled tissue back to see the rest. A fancy smart phone greeted her. "Oh, my!"

"He doesn't want you going without a phone. I told him yours hasn't worked right since the ladder mishap." Neither did Ian. "I'll show you how to use it. It's already activated and ready. The lock code is Caleb's birthday."

She smiled. "Clever." Yips sounded from the couch. They turned to find Tia on the floor on all fours, facing the roly-poly pup, also on all fours attempting play. "He's so little."

"He won't be for long." Ian gave a wry look. He indicated three identically wrapped gifts on Bri's wagon-wheel coffee table. "Those are to you, me and Tia, from Kate."

Bri helped Tia set Mistletoe in the basket, where he cuddled into a ball, clearly worn out and ready for a nap. Tia straightened his pawprint blanket and rested three fingers on top of his forehead, then kissed his cheek and muttered under her breath. Ian looked to Bri and raised his brows.

"Um, I didn't realize she noticed this, but when she lies down for her nap and is almost asleep, I brush my fingertips along her forehead, say prayers over her and kiss her cheek."

Tenderness swept through Ian. Bri seemed to be getting attached to Tia quickly, and Tia to Bri. "Shall we?" He passed out Kate's gifts. "Kate said you and I have to open ours together," he said to Bri, but nodded to Tia. "Have at it."

Tia tore into hers and squealed. "A *Fairytown* DVD!"

"Ready?" Bri poked a finger in her paper.

"Hey, no cheating. She said open them at the same time." As Ian spoke, though, ripping sounded from his. "Oops." He grinned.

"Unconvincing." She ripped open her paper, as did he.

They both gasped. Then frowned. Heavily.

Ian stared at the identical *Beauty and the Beast* DVDs and sighed. Bri awkwardly nibbled her lip, and didn't know what to say.

He shook his head and set the disk aside. Upside down, so the front image depicting Belle and Beast dancing wouldn't show.

"Kate's a mess," Bri commented, shoving her disk in between her couch cushions, away from

Tia, which almost made Ian laugh. The feeling had been so foreign to him for the past two years.

At least he and Bri were on the same page, knowing how utterly ridiculous their friends and family were being by trying to match the two of them together. Ian stood. "Tia, I have another surprise for you." Ian pulled out the cookie cutters. He'd stuck the mix in Bri's fridge earlier.

Tia rose and approached cautiously. "What's that for?"

"Well, I hear you can make Christmas tree ornaments out of cookies. Would you like to?"

Tia smiled shyly, but grabbed Bri's hand instead of his. "Can we?"

Bri tried to steer Tia toward Ian. "Of course. Your dad bought it so you two could make them together."

Tia frowned. "I'd rather make them with you."

Ouch. "I'd like to help, if it's okay."

"I guess so." Tia didn't look or sound convincing.

Midway into cookie making, Ian's emergency beeper sounded. He read the message, then eyed Bri, then Tia. "Sweetie, it looks like you'll get to bake with Miss Bri, after all. Daddy has to go to work." He faced Bri's questioning glance. "We have an incoming air trauma. Ten minutes out. Can you watch Tia?"

"Be happy to."

Ian bent to hug Tia and, while she stiffened, he didn't miss the disappointment brewing deep in her eyes. "Sorry, Tia."

"It doesn't matter." She scowled.

While her tone attested to that, the pain in her eyes betrayed it.

Chapter Seven

"Miss Bri, what's that sound?" Tia scrambled from sitting near Mistletoe's basket to standing.

"It's a helicopter landing at the trauma center."

"Oh. Is he helping that person?"

"Yes." Bri let the curtain fall back as Ian and his crew met the flight medics rushing the stretcher their way.

"Oh." Tia nodded. Then went back to playing with the pup.

"Your dad has a very important job, you know. He saves people's lives for a living."

"But his job is supposed to be a dad, too."

"He's still your dad, even when he's at work."

"It doesn't seem like it." She shrugged. "He promised to work less. But he works a lot. My mom breaks promises, too."

"When did your dad tell you he'd work less?"

"At Make-A-Zoo."

"Give him a chance, Tia. I really think your

dad is the kind of person who keeps his promises." Watching Ian through the window, and having seen how much Tia meant to him, Bri was sure. Grouchy or not, Ian was a good dad. A bit of a worry wart, though, which reminded Bri— "Hey, Tia, how would you like to learn to swim?"

She sucked in air. "In the lake?"

"No. We never, ever go in the lake. It's dirty and stinky with fish. And Lem got bitten by a snake last summer. So never, ever go to the lake alone, okay?"

She nodded sagely. "Where will we swim?"

"I have a huge hot tub in my sunroom. I'll turn down the heat so it'll be safe for you. It has bubbles that feel good against your back. You'll love it."

"I don't have a swimsuit."

"Do you have shorts and a T-shirt at your house?"

She nodded, started for the door then looked back at Mistletoe. Bri smiled. "He can go with us." Bri bundled up Tia and the puppy and they walked across the lot to Lakeview, the road next to the trauma center leading to Ian's.

Once back, Bri set Mistletoe in his basket next to the hot tub, changed into her swimsuit and helped Tia in.

"You swim good!" Tia said as Bri taught her to tread water.

"I was a lifeguard growing up. I give swim lessons to kids." Within two hours, Bri had Tia swimming over and under the water. "You're like a little fish. Good job, Tia."

"Not a fish. A mermaid fairy, silly."

"Oh, excuse me. You're a mermaid fairy, are you?"

Tia giggled. Hugged Bri. "I like you. I'm glad you're my babysitter."

"I like you, too. I'm glad I'm your babysitter."

Tia eyed her with longing. "I really wish…" Tia trailed off. The wistful look disappeared into a face that looked too scared to hope. But for what? What had Tia been about to say?

A part of Bri decided she might be better off not knowing. They got out and dried off.

Carrying the contented puppy extra carefully, Tia went to the window where Bri had watched the helicopter land hours ago. "I wonder if that person is okay now?"

"I wonder that, too."

"What do you think happened to them?"

"I'm not sure. But I am sure that, since your dad is taking care of them, they're in the best hands possible."

"Grandma told me to pray when I see a ambulance."

"That's a good idea."

"Is the helicopter a ambulance with fairy wings?"

Bri smiled. "Sort of. Would you like to pray for the person who was inside it?"

Tia nodded, and Bri led them through a prayer for God to help the trauma crew save whoever had been brought. Remembering her mom's passing on a holiday, Bri realized that for one local family, Christmas Day would either end in miracle or tragedy.

Eagle Point was a small town. Likely she knew the person.

While they didn't have a local newspaper, Eagle Point did have four young men who'd started *Four Guys, a Dog and a Blog.* An up-to-the-minute live newsfeed of local happenings. It was more reliable than the news. Bri didn't want to get on the computer with Tia here, though. She'd check later, or ask Ian.

Regardless, her heart went out to whoever had been in that helicopter. And for the loved ones probably frantic with worry and fear now.

She prayed for this family that hope would prevail over tragedy.

Another drowning victim.

This one, a toddler at a Christmas party where everyone thought someone else was watching him. They'd saved his life...but barely. Monstrous, pulsating fear gripped Ian that Bri's deck was only yards away from Eagle Point Lake.

Compounding it was the fact that his parents had an unfenced pond in their yard. He'd tell them to either put a fence up or drain the pond before next weekend, when his mom asked to have Tia.

Seeing that child come in gray and lifeless today made Ian long to rush home—to Bri's, rather—hug Tia and never let go. Every day was a day he'd never get back with her and he'd missed far too much time already. "Mitch, I need to cut back on hours. At least one day a week for Tia."

Mitch nodded, understanding in his eyes. "I'll see what I can do." Ian left, his feet moving like NASCAR wheels over asphalt to Bri's cabin. He knocked. No answer. He knocked again.

And again. Harder. Had Bri taken pain meds and fallen asleep? Tia had figured out the locks that day at Ellie's, which meant she could figure out Bri's, too. Heart pounding, fear coursing through him, Ian pushed open the door. "Hello?"

No answer. Total dead silence.

He ran through the house, then outside. Silence greeted him there, too, beneath a sepia sunset. Its muted glow hid behind thick, gunmetal clouds brewing a winter storm and causing the lake to look as dull and lifeless as that little boy's eyes.

Then suddenly, unexplainably, he'd improved. Started breathing on his own. Mitch called it amazing.

Little boy was on a ventilator still, but because

someone at home knew CPR, Ian was confident the little guy would make it. Hopefully without brain problems from lack of oxygen.

Ian's thoughts drove him into a sheer panic. Silence entombed the lake. The yard. The house. Fear gripped his chest like a vise, making it hard to pull air into his lungs. He rushed down Bri's deck steps and relaxed a measure when he saw no one near the lake. Unless...

He walked faster, around the lake's edge.

Unless Bri had fallen asleep and Tia wandered off. "Tia? Bri?" Ian fought pandemonium inside his mind.

He jogged back up Bri's deck steps, calling their names. He walked briskly through her living room to a sunroom. Relief washed over him when he heard a woman's voice mingle with a child's giggle, then raucous laughter. Wait. Tia actually *laughing?* This he had to see. He followed the sounds of singsongs, laughter...

And splashing? Yes. He definitely heard splashing.

He rounded the corner and froze.

Tia and Bri were shoulder deep in a big, bubbly hot tub, face-to-face, playing some kind of clapping game and singing.

He stepped down the skid-free sunroom tile. "Tia?" Where was her life jacket? How was she staying afloat?

The pair stopped singing and eyed him with frozen expressions, which made him realize he needed to cool his jets.

Bri waved from the hot tub. "Hi." She raised her casted arm, demonstrating that she'd covered the cast in plastic and taped the ends to keep water from getting inside. As if she was afraid he'd scold her.

Tia splashed to the edge nearest him. "I can swim! Miss Bri learned me!" Tia scrambled up the steps, dripping water on the aqua-blue tile.

"Taught," Bri corrected. Then stood and got out of the hot tub, as well.

Bri's cheeks tinged pink until she grabbed her robe and shrugged it on, belting it at her waist.

Ian focused on helping Tia with her towel. "Where are your arm floaty things?" He looked around.

"I don't need them. Miss Bri taught me how to swim. I can even go in over my head and stay there as long as a fish!"

If that was supposed to make Ian feel better, it didn't. He rose as Bri approached him, eyeing him with determination.

She leaned in, presumably to be out of Tia's earshot, and said, "Take a chill pill, Ian. I was a lifeguard and swim instructor every summer until two years ago when Mom got sick."

He nodded. Calmed himself down. Tried not

to notice how deep the water level was on that hot tub, and how the temperature could easily dehydrate a child Tia's size.

He'd discuss that with Bri later.

But, of course, she'd know, having a child-care degree. Sure enough, a glimpse at the thermometer read a safe level for children. Bri must've turned the heat down. He met her gaze.

Hers was solemn but understanding. "I knew how bad it scared you when you realized how close I am to the lake and when you learned she couldn't swim." She peeled the plastic off her arm.

Ian discarded it for her, listening as she continued.

"You don't need to stress. She needs to learn, in case she ever encounters water and doesn't understand the danger. Or happens to be at a pool party and accidentally falls in."

Like the toddler today.

Ian nodded, respect blooming anew for her. "You're right. It's better she learn to swim than for me to keep her shielded from water. Sorry."

"I understand. Your concern means you care. She gets that."

He eyed Tia, dressing into a clean set of clothes. "How did you get those?"

Bri shrugged. "Tia said you leave a key under your planter. We took a walk to your place. It was good exercise. Besides, Tia wanted to see where you worked again, so I walked her by there and showed her."

"Thanks for watching her, Bri. And for teaching her to safely swim. I also appreciate being able to depend on you for night calls."

"My pleasure. I figured with you being the only anesthesiologist, that you have to go in. Can you tell me what happened to the person who came in?"

"You don't want to know. But he made it."

"That's good. I'm glad you're a doctor, Ian. I know how you helped me the day of the ladder mishap." Kindness and respect in her eyes made him forget what they were even talking about. When was the last time he'd seen those two things reflected toward him in a woman's eyes? Not for a long time.

"Speaking of ladder mishap, I determined what caused it."

"I'm all ears, not that I'll ever climb it when alone," she said ruefully, while helping Tia dry her hair. Mistletoe chewed on the end of Tia's towel. Ian almost smiled at the puppy's antics.

Then stopped himself. He refused to get attached to it.

Or to Bri. Yet he had a feeling it was too late. Especially if she kept feeding him compliments and that pup kept flashing him soulful puppy eyes the color of the hazelnut coffee he loved so much.

Ian faced Bri. "You placed the ladder in the path of trickling water on a day the temperature dropped to thirty-two degrees Fahrenheit."

Bri grew quiet. She'd frozen, as the water must have under her ladder's legs that day. "So that's what caused it to slide?"

He nodded. "Seems you set the ladder on concrete, below a lawn hose dribbling water downhill."

Her whole face lit up like a lightbulb moment. "Yes. I had the hose dripping to try and save it from freezing and cracking." She nibbled her lip. "But it seems I cracked my arm instead. Not too smart, huh?"

"I think you're very smart. I think you just had a lot on your mind that led to a momentary lapse in judgment."

She reached for a casserole from her fridge. Ian helped her put it in the oven. "It smells like pure culinary delight."

"I made extra so you'd have a couple of servings. I wasn't sure if you'd make it back in time to make dinner for you and Tia, so I took care of dinner for you." She rubbed her nose. Her voice warbled a bit. "The meal is—was—Mom's Christmas casserole. It's like a shepherd's pie in

Christmas colors, green beans and tomato sauce for… I'm blathering. Sorry."

He shook his head. "It's perfectly okay. I know you miss her." Ian had the strongest urge to tug her in for a hug. But his arms wouldn't work. Besides that, she might take it the wrong way. She cleared her throat twice, which was when he realized she fought tears. "Tough day."

And before he knew it, he'd wrapped an arm around her and hauled her in close. She blinked surprise and stiffened. He gave her a quick squeeze and let her go.

He took a healthy step back, emotions churning inside at the core of who he was.

Almost as though the hug, fast as it was, had bolstered him as much as it had her. Emotion thickened in her eyes. "Thanks."

"You're good with children, Bri," he said to her.

She blinked, all befuddled, as if she'd never heard a compliment before.

"Thanks, Ian. Considering I want to be a mom someday, that helps."

"You'll make a good one."

Her face grew so welcoming it reminded him of coming home to the crackle of a warm fireplace and a rich cup of hot cocoa.

Looking into her eyes felt like sinking his teeth into inch-thick caramel on the sweetest apple in the world. He looked around and realized she and Tia actually had made candy apples that probably matched Bri's sweet demeanor.

Her entire character opened up like literal arms of friendship. Her hospitable personality mesmerized like a superlit haven on a dark night in a dismal sea. And all he wanted to do was drift toward it. Toward her.

Ian blinked away the images. The silly notions and the need for more moments like this. He didn't have time for cozy. And he didn't have the heart to dream anymore. Not for himself.

He only wanted to make life better for Tia and give her the love, protection and security she so badly needed and deserved.

Tia rushed up in a multi-colored tutu brighter than Sully's rainbow sherbet. "Tia, how many of those things do you have, anyway?" She wore a different one every day.

"It's what Mommy always bought me with your birthday money. Every tutu I have is 'cause of you."

Surprise went through him. Wow. All the checks he'd sent hadn't gone to waste.

"So you got the cards I sent?"

Tia looked away. "Sorta. I found them in the trash where she threw them away…along with pretty pictures I drawed her." Tia's face looked as if she were unsure she should've shared that.

Anger boiled inside Ian, but he tamped it down for Tia's sake. He dipped his face to her eye level. "Hey, it's okay."

Tia shook her head. "No. It's not."

Smart kid. Not that he was bragging or proud or anything. Ian's chest swelled. "I'm sorry about the cards. I'm just glad you got the money."

"I'm sorry, too."

"Hey, kiddo. You have nothing to be sorry about. None of this is your fault. Okay?"

She eyed him ashamedly, almost sheepish. "I meant I'm sorry I didn't know."

Know what? That he cared? That he'd sent gifts every week for years and extravagant things for holidays? Letters at least three times a week? Did she know any of it?

Or had Ava trashed it all and led his daughter to assume he never thought of her? She was all he could think about. Then and now. Did she know he loved her more than anything on earth? Did she know?

He scrubbed a hand over her hair. "You will."

Ian's eyes veered to Bri's fridge, where Tia's artwork was displayed. He felt a twinge of jealousy that Bri had received Tia's handiwork ahead of him. But her artwork, like her trust, was something he was going to have to figure out how to earn.

Chapter Eight

"Do you think he'll like it?" Tia asked Bri at her coffee table the day after Christmas, shortly after Ian dropped her off.

Bri smiled at Tia's colored-pencil masterpiece and recalled Ian looking wistfully at the artwork hanging on her fridge. "I'm certain he will love it."

"Do you even know what it is?" Tia's gaze narrowed.

"Um, well, that's a stand of trees."

"They're naked. Just like yours."

Bri yelped a laugh. "Tia, we shouldn't say that word."

"Why? It only means they don't got their leaves."

"Have." So that's why Tia had told Boom about her trees. Bri hadn't noticed Tia talking to Boom as much since getting Mistletoe. Bri eyed the pup, curled by the fireplace, paws prancing in his sleep.

"The air looks funny outside." Tia went to Bri's window.

"They say it might snow."

Tia whirled. "Yay! I hope so. I love snow!"

"Really? What a coincidence! I do, too."

Bri went to look outside and saw Ian's truck pulling up the drive. "Your dad's here."

"He's not much like a dad." Yet Tia scrambled to finish her picture, anyway. Bri wished Tia would refer to him as Dad more. Only when her defenses were down did Bri ever hear her say it. "Tia, I like when you refer to him as your dad. I wish—"

"Block him!" Tia shot to the playroom puppet stage with the paper and box of coloring utensils.

Bri laughed. "You mean stall him? He's too big to block." The thought of trying to keep the tall, dark and heavily muscled ex-military guy back even an inch humored Bri.

Bri's new phone rang. Ian's handsome face displayed on the screen, making Bri grin. She realized that he'd taken time to load her phone and put himself as the emergency contact. Undoubtedly so no one would call Caleb while deployed. Ian's thoughtfulness warmed her heart. She wasn't the only one Ian was protecting.

Bri tried to keep the smile and emotion out of

her voice as she swiped the answer function as he'd shown her. "Hello?"

"Hey, is Tia close by?"

Bri noticed some of the curt formality had seeped from his tone, replaced by hints of kindness and familiarity. For reasons she didn't want to indulge, that observation widened the smile she was trying to stave. "She's occupied at the moment. Need her?"

"I cut out of the trauma center early. Went to town and picked up Jonah."

"Awesome!"

"Yeah, so if you could make sure the pup is put up, I'll bring the fish in. Maybe we'll let one of them stay at your place, so we don't have an accidental, traumatic lunch."

Bri giggled. "Yes, that would be horrible. I'll keep either one, whichever's easier on you. Although it might be better to keep Mistletoe here, since a fish won't chew up a sofa over being left alone longer than he thinks he should."

Ian's chuckle wended its way around her heart like his hug the other day. She steeled herself against its effects. "I see you at the door now. I'll let you go."

She hung up and scooped Mistletoe up, then let Ian in. His hand snaked out as if he was about to scratch the puppy under his chin. Then he recoiled and scowled. Bri snickered. "He starting to get to you, Ian?"

His eyes rose slowly from the dog to her. The look in his eyes glued her to the spot. Then, just as fast as that look swept in, it was gone, replaced by a look as harsh as a blustery winter wind.

Bri set Mistletoe in the kennel Ian had in his other hand. She decided not to comment on the fact that Ian had picked out plush purple bedding and several colorful chew toys the size of Mistletoe's mouth. The puppy jumped on the toys.

Their squeaking brought Tia's face out of the puppet tent. "Oh!" She scrambled out and ran to the house, paper in her hand. She eyed Ian in a state of little-girl shock. "You got him his very own house?"

Ian nodded at Tia, then nodded at the table behind her.

Tia slowly turned, then surged to her feet, squealing. "You got my fishy!" She leaned close to the tank and watched the betta swim around his castle. "Hi, Jonah! Welcome home." She blinked and frowned. "Wait! What if Mistletoe tries to bite him?"

"We thought of that. It might be best if you separated them for now. Keep the pup here and the fish at our house."

"Well, Mistletoe does need a lot more petting."

"You know not to pet Jonah, though, right?"

Tia nodded. "Okay." She peered on the floor. "Oh! I almost forgot." She bent and swept up the paper and pressed it to her tummy, as if suddenly nervous. She approached her dad. "I made this for you. It's a squirrel family, like we got at Build-A-Zoo."

Ian took the paper, true emotion lighting his eyes. Bri looked away.

"Thank you, Tia. It's beautiful." He hugged her, and surprisingly, she let him, although she wiggled free quickly. "Although it's very, very pretty, it's not as beautiful as you."

Tia giggled. Then grew serious. "Do you think Miss Bri is pretty, too?"

Awkward. Bri didn't dare look at Ian.

But he sure looked at her. She could see the look of astonishing respect and gratitude that felt a little too close to adoration. She briefly met his gaze, then looked away. But he didn't. He stared at her.

And grinned.

Boy, oh, boy, if this prince had any more charm, she was in trouble. Bri decided she'd much rather contend with his brooding.

Tia tugged his sleeve. "Well? Do you?"

Ian cleared his throat. Shifted his feet. "Your babysitter is very pretty."

Bri didn't miss Ian's emphasis to Tia on *baby-sitter*.

She was thankful he had wisdom and foresight to handle such uncomfortable conversations and awkward situations.

"I have Brock coming over in a bit to help me knock out that second cabin. We're a couple days away from finishing that one and starting on the third."

Which would put them two days ahead of schedule. "I hope nothing happens to ruin how well things are going."

Ian interacted with Tia for a bit. "I need to work on Miss Bri's cabin, but I'll see you in a bit, okay?"

Tia stiffened and leaned away from his attempted hug.

Bri felt bad for keeping him from time with Tia.

Looking frustrated and downtrodden, Ian nodded a departure to Bri and met Brock at cabin three.

"Miss Bri?" Tia said an hour later. "You know that snow we said we wished we were getting? I think it's here."

Bri went to the window, shocked to see gray-white flakes falling from the sky. Until her nose caught whiffs of something much more ominous. Not snow. Ashes. Acrid. Close.

"Tia, put Mistletoe in his cage. And quickly put your shoes on, please." Bri grabbed Tia's coat and the fish and headed them for the nearest door farthest from the smoke.

Something was on fire.

By the time Bri rushed outside, Ian and Brock were sprinting up the road. Bri turned and nearly passed out.

"Miss Bri, your lodge is burning." Tia's eyes bulged.

Bri grabbed Tia and moved her toward Ian's truck. "I know." She put Tia inside so the smoke wouldn't get to her, then dialed.

"Nine-one-one. What is your emergency?"

"I need the fire department right away. My lodge, Landis Lodge at Eagle Point Lake, is fully engulfed in flames."

"Miss Landis, we received another call on it. We have units en route. Are you inside or near the building?"

"No." Bri felt like throwing up. She couldn't watch, but she couldn't look away. She set the phone in her seat, buckled Tia into the backseat belt of the king cab then pulled Ian's truck to the trauma center so the fire trucks could get through.

"Ma'am?" said a voice from her seat.

Bri snatched up the phone. "Excuse me, I'm sorry. What?"

"I need to know if there is anyone inside?"

"N-no. But please tell the trucks to hurry."

"They're moving as fast as they can. Is someone with you?"

"Sort of. Dr. Shupe and his friend ran toward it. Looks like they have a garden hose and fire extinguishers on it, but the fire looks too big." Bri's words came out in huge gulps.

"I'm scared," came from the backseat. Tia clutched Mistletoe, who must've picked up on their fright because he'd started to softly paw Tia and whimper.

"I need to go." Bri could hear sirens now and she needed to get control of herself and help calm Tia down. Comfort her.

Dear God, Dear God was all Bri could pray as the flames licked trees overhanging the lodge.

If those dry branches caught fire, it would spread and burn down every single cabin on her property.

Bri put the car in Reverse and went to take Tia to the trauma center. Employees poured out of it as the fire trucks pulled in. Kate rushed Bri. "Ian called me. Is everyone okay?"

Bri nodded, tried to help unbuckle Tia, but her hands trembled. Kate took over. Tia reached for

Bri, tears bubbling in her eyes. Bri held her close. "It's going to be okay, Tia."

"But my daddy. The fire is very big."

Bri held her closer. "He'll be careful. The firemen are there. They won't let him get hurt. Your dad is very smart. He won't put himself in danger. Okay?"

"But he wants to save your lodge. I do, too."

Bri almost burst into tears. "Things can be replaced. Things will work out. It will be okay. God will take care of me." Bri's voice broke on the sentence, but not her hope.

Mitch had already climbed behind the wheel of Ian's truck, and some male trauma center employees jumped in the back. Driving to the cabin would be faster.

Kate's female coworkers grabbed the fish, Tia and the dog and swept Bri inside so she couldn't see the now-raging fire burn her mother's dreams to the ground.

"This couldn't have happened at a worse time." Ian tossed his sooty insulated gloves on his desk in the trauma center. Four hours the department had battled the blaze. They'd saved much of the lodge, but the entire west end of it was gone.

Mitch sat with his face in his hands. "She can rebuild."

"Not in time for the bank. That first cabin has

extensive water damage, not to mention the heat blew its windows out, melted the electrical and charred the wood. It's not livable. We'll have to tear it down and build it from scratch."

Pressure sat on Ian's chest along with a sick, horrible feeling. "I can't see any way now that she'll make the bank's renovation deadlines."

Especially since two hours before the fire, his second nurse-anesthetist had informed them her formerly laid-off husband had gotten a job and she was moving in four days.

Then Lisa, his only other nurse-anesthetist, in her second trimester of pregnancy, had started cramping in surgery and was now on bed rest as of this afternoon.

That left Ian.

The pressure starting to get to him, Ian began to pace. "I can't catch a break." Ian shook his head, then immediately went into problem-solving mode. "What I need is about six more hours in a day. We all do."

"We'll just call in longer-term recruits. See if Refuge physicians and the PJs will come rotate between shifts helping at the trauma center and also with the cabins."

"I know we can count on the PJs, but they're in a training op for the next two weeks. Meanwhile, her lodge is exposed to everything under the sun. It's too big to tarp."

"We'll figure something out, Shupe." Mitch rose, clapped a hand on Ian's shoulder. Then bent his head. Ian realized Mitch was praying whether Ian wanted him to or not. He'd done it on a few occasions overseas when things were going south with Ava.

A sense of peace descended despite the circumstances. It calmed the whirlwind inside Ian's mind. "This makes no sense," Ian blurted.

Mitch lifted his eyes but not his hand. "What's that?"

"This—this feeling of well-being amid tragedy and stress."

"Just receive it, man." Mitch went to praying again.

And for once, Ian wasn't about to argue. Not with the prayer, not with the person praying.

"You need to pray for Bri, too. She's at wits' end." Ian eyed Mitch after the prayer.

"Got it covered. Kate's there now. Lauren's rounding up staff from Refuge to help us at the center."

"Thanks, man. I hate that it's always me being the needy one." At once, Ian understood Bri's struggle with needing help and being vulnerable.

"You uprooted your life to help me open this trauma center, Ian. You've helped me through more than you know, just by being you. You're stalwart and strong. Steady and dependable."

Ian punched Mitch in the arm. "You're my BFF, too."

Mitch burst out laughing. Shoved Ian and they left the lounge with staff eyeing them peculiarly.

Ian's phone rang as he sat. "Hey, Bri. Everything okay?"

She drew a ragged breath. "Tia's fine."

"You?"

"I called the loan officer. He accused me of arson."

"What?" Ian surged to his feet. "That's ridiculous!"

"Yeah, well apparently he's already talked to the insurance company to see if I had anything recently upgraded. The agent was a good friend of Mom's and gave me a heads-up that the loan officer is snooping around. Why does he want to shut me down?"

"I have a pretty good idea." Ian had seen a dark sedan with out-of-town plates at the bank on a regular basis. Lem had, too, and had told Ian the guy was a land developer. "I don't have proof yet, but put it this way—the loan company won't benefit from your lodge. He's a known shark. He would benefit, however, from leveling the lodge and building a subdivision on the lake."

Bri sighed. "I suspected as much."

"I need to do a routine surgery, then a last set of patient rounds, then I'll be over."

"Have you eaten dinner? I was getting ready to cook."

"Actually, no, but don't cook. You need a break. Let me take you and Tia out for a nice dinner at Golden Terrace."

"I—"

"Don't. You're not a charity case. You are my favorite babysitter, though. So, how 'bout it. You up for a steak?"

"Are you kidding me? I'll take two, please." Her sentence ended in a laugh, causing Ian to grin, too. "I hope Tia picks up on your resiliency, Bri. It's a life lesson that a lot of people don't have."

"Thanks, Ian." The emotion in her voice caused a softening inside him. For once, he was conflicted about fighting it. "See you in a couple of hours, barring any more traumas."

"Or freak fires."

"That you *definitely* didn't start. We'll get that cleared up ASAP, Bri. Don't fret over it, okay?"

"Thanks for believing in me, Ian."

"I'll see you in a while."

He brushed a thumb over Bri's photo icon in his phone contacts. "Thanks for putting up with me." While he'd already disconnected, and knew she wouldn't hear, he needed to say the words, anyway. If to no one else than himself.

Ian walked toward the O.R. area with many thoughts dawning.

As soon as Mitch had prayed for Ian, he'd not only caught a case of the strangest sense of peace, he'd come to an instant understanding that failures didn't define a person, only whether the person pressed on in the midst of them.

A person like Bri. And yet even she was about to break.

He brushed another finger over her picture, wishing he could send her strength and perseverance through the phone.

"You always stand at scrub sinks fondling phones, Shupe?"

Ian looked up. Two PJs and a third young man stood in scrubs, grinning. "Hey, Brock. Manny." Ian shook their hands.

"This is my stepson, Javier. He's been away at Superman school." Manny indicated the young man who grinned at the words.

"Javier, nice to meet you. Wow, Superman school, huh?" Ian knew that was a training phase in the pararescue course. "Following in the old man's footsteps, huh?"

Javier laughed, jabbed Manny's stout ribs. "Old man's right." Javier nodded to Ian's phone. "So, you gonna keep playing FarmVille on that thing or put us to work or what?"

Ian laughed. "Razz me all you want. We appreciate you guys coming to help us out. But I thought you left on a training op today, though?"

Brock grinned. Nodded at a pretty nurse. "Hey, this trauma center's hopping. That's training. Besides, Lauren called us about the lodge gal's fire. Tragic. So we came back to help."

Ian nodded. "We could use the help rebuilding, too."

"Say no more. We'll take care of calling in recruits. Like an old-fashioned barn raising. Involve both communities."

Ian knew that meant Refuge and Eagle Point.

He realized that Mitch's prayer for God to send help just showed up in the form of a team of special operations airmen. "Thanks, guys. Really."

Thanks to You, too, up there, Big Guy, Ian thought but couldn't say.

Bri was going to need more help than she'd probably ever needed in her life. The question remained whether she would set aside her wounded pride and let people help. That would make the difference in her lodge retreat making it. Or not.

Chapter Nine

"Did you have a nice time at Golden Terrace last night?" Kate handed Bri woodsy trim for cabin table-runners they were making.

"Yes. The food was excellent."

Kate eyed Bri over her iced tea glass rim. "I meant did you have a nice time…with Ian."

Bri scowled. "I was more focused on the steak."

Kate smirked. "Interested to know if he had a good time?"

"No."

"Then I won't tell you about how he grinned like a crazy person the entire time he talked about it before surgery this morning."

Bri politely ignored Kate. And little jumps her pulse took with every word of Kate's. A car pulled up outside.

"Lauren's back." Kate went to get the door.

Bri stood up to see Tia, in the other room crawling around the rug, pawing and snorting.

Lauren came in and giggled. "Either she's a very small bear or a very large June bug." Lauren set fringed material next to the sewing machine. Then unfurled a large quilt.

"It's gorgeous!" Bri exclaimed. "Who made it?"

"The quilt-club ladies from church. They're making five more—six if you'd like one for your cabin."

"I'd hate to burden them—"

"She'd love a quilt, thanks." Kate grinned. "One of these days, girl, we are going to break you of that indebtedness."

"But I *am* a burden…to everyone."

"And there are bound to be times in our lives when we need help, too. Then it'll be your turn to help us." Lauren set about sewing decorative fringe on cabin rugs. "Besides, that's the quilt-ladies' ministry. They delight in doing it."

Bri hadn't asked them to do all this, but it would save a ton of money and Lauren loved to sew. "I'm glad you're a professional seamstress in addition to being a stellar nurse."

Lauren smiled. "I heard he was prepared to buy you two."

"Who?"

Lauren grinned, and winked at Kate. "Ian. Steaks."

Bri groaned and bumped her forehead on the

sewing table. "You're worse than Kate." Bri shot Kate a look. "Did you recruit her to your match-making club or something?" Bri asked in low tones, since Tia crawled in the room and was now within earshot.

At least the women had sense enough to be cautious with Tia around. Yips sounded. Tia and Mistletoe played tug-of-war with a tiny yellow-and-red-striped rope.

Lauren unfurled fringed shower curtains she'd sewn. "Like?"

"Love! Those are pretty." Bri appreciated the company and knew they were keeping her mind off things. Such as the fact that the main lodge next to her personal cabin was now a charred-out shell. Water damage from the fire trucks had caused as much damage as the smoke, heat and flames.

Suddenly something at the window caught Bri's eye. She gasped, surged up, bumped her arm and cried out in pain.

Lauren and Kate rushed to where she'd stumbled to the window, hyperventilating at this point. "More ash!"

Bri ran outside at the sight of it. Had it caught fire again? Her hyperventilating calmed when she realized that this time it really was snow. She instantly felt ridiculous as her friends gathered around her. "Bri, it's okay. It's stress."

"I feel like an idiot."

"You're not," Kate said. Lauren turned to tend to Tia, then came to see what the commotion was. Bri eyed the sky, and the white powder that fell. "The guys can't renovate the cabins in this."

"Yes, they can. Somewhat. Snow is good. Southern Illinois snow rarely falls or lasts for more than a day. Plus, it'll keep any hidden embers from reigniting." Kate rubbed the chill from Bri's arms. "We'll get you through this, Bri. Okay?"

She nodded but felt like a fraud doing it, because absolutely nothing was going to convince her things would be okay.

She peered outside, through gray clouds, finally getting how Ian could question God. She wasn't inclined to doubt God's goodness, just whether she was meant to let go of the lodge.

Caleb told her that would be easiest. And that was before the fire. "I hope Ian didn't somehow get word to Caleb and tell him. He'd really worry."

Kate and Lauren didn't confirm or deny Caleb knowing or Ian informing, and that didn't make her feel good.

While Lauren had Tia in the kitchen, Bri sat on a rug across from Kate and put her chin on her knees. *I don't want to take the easy way, Lord. But I don't want to waste everyone's time, either.*

This lodge is a problem for too many people. "Kate, what if Lisa started contracting because she had to take Ian's load plus the other anesthesiologist's? He needs time with Tia to cultivate trust. I'm hindering all that."

"No, Bri. It's just a rough patch in your life right now. A bottleneck of stress always squeezes the most right before things push through."

"I don't understand how a person's life can rain fire and snow in the same day." Bri put her head down since someone entered. If it was Lauren, Bri didn't want to upset Tia.

Kate's fingers resting slightly on her shoulder caused tears to break through. "I'll never make the bank's deadline."

The hand felt herculean strong. Whoa. Not Kate. Bri looked up to find Ian's tormented gaze locked on hers. His jaw was tense and empathy generated from his eyes.

"Where's everyone?" Bri and Ian were alone in the room.

"I sent them to the sunroom." He pulled her to her feet and held her up against him. She shouldn't, but she let herself lean into his strength, and let the tears flow.

He held her for several moments until all Bri could hear was his calm breathing and her jagged pulls. Yet, she sensed something was wrong.

She leaned back. "Ian, what's up?" Foreboding encroached on her.

"One of my PJ buddy's wives is driving Tia to my mom's for a couple or few days."

"Why?" Bri's heart thumped in her chest. "I can still watch her—"

His finger touched her lips, which silenced and surprised her. So much so that she startled and backed away. He looked confused, then slightly annoyed and confused again.

Something was wrong.

Really, really wrong.

"Ian, what's going on?"

He tensed. Eyes flickered with something she couldn't define yet it scared her to death. She braced his arms. "You're trembling." His breathing had turned shallow, and he averted his gaze.

What on earth? Had he lost a patient? No, he'd lost patients before and had never reacted like this.

At some point, Lauren had taken Tia to the car—Bri could see them getting in, Tia packing Mistletoe and Lauren Tia's suitcase. Finally, he seemed to be able to speak.

"There's no way you can watch her with everything you have going on. I have stuff going on, too. Mom wanted her for this weekend, anyway, and was delighted to get her early. I hadn't sent her there before now because I was trying to build my own relationship with her."

"It'll happen, Ian."

"Not if life keeps throwing us curveballs."

Bri's heart sank. "I don't expect your help with the lodge. Please don't take time away from Tia to work on it. Promise me you won't. She needs you more than I do. Uh, my lodge."

"I can't promise that."

Bri shook her head. "Ian, you can never get back this time."

"Trust me, I'm fully aware of that."

Bri's heart soared. "Wait! Mom had to have had insurance." Unless she'd grown too ill to think about bills and let it lapse. *Please let there be insurance.* "Caleb would probably know."

Ian's jaw spasmed at mention of her brother's name. "Ian? What's wrong? What are you not telling me?"

He backed her to the couch and sat her down. He knelt in front of her. His hands trembled as he squeezed her arms. Emotion and determination glinted in his eyes. "Caleb's unit was ambushed."

She was going to pass out.

"Watch her arm," Ian instructed Kate, who protected Bri's head as her body slinked and her knees gave way.

"I'll get a cool cloth." Kate rushed to the

kitchen. Ian rested Bri's head in his lap. Her eyes were open but wide and dazed. Unblinking. "Bri, can you hear me?"

She blinked as if barely seeing. "Think so."

Completely disoriented. "Has she eaten today?"

"Yes. It's probably hypotension from emotional trauma." Kate met Ian's gaze. "What did you say to her? Does she know you got word to Caleb?"

Ian's jaw clenched. "No." He met and held her gaze. "Two hours after that message got through, Caleb's unit was ambushed. He was the point man."

Kate's face paled. She eyed him, then Bri. "Is he—?" she whispered.

"No word."

About that time, Bri sat up. Gripped Ian with weak fists. "You have to go find him."

Her words clutched him to the core. Ian felt responsible. Yet Caleb's name was the one on all of the insurance paperwork. "I had no choice but to call."

Who was he trying to convince? Himself? Or Bri?

Because right now, neither one of them looked convinced he hadn't just made a mistake that could have cost Bri's brother his life.

Yet he'd done what he thought best.

Bri sat, knees curled under her. "What are they doing to find him?" She sipped the water Kate brought but violently pushed away the granola bar extended.

"They've sent teams of SEALs. Some PJs are going, too, among others. Brock's C.O. pulled in some favors."

When Bri lifted her gaze, her eyes were void of everything other than anger. "Did you tell him about the fire?"

Ian held her gaze. "Yes. His command post, anyway."

Her teeth clenched. "Would they have gotten the message through no matter what? No matter the danger?"

"Most likely." He wasn't about to make excuses. To tell her he'd had to call to help get insurance money moving for the lodge. In light of her brother, his noble efforts seemed in vain.

She swallowed. Slipped from his reach. Shook her head. Looked as though she wasn't sure whether to beat him up or cry on his shoulder. Ian couldn't bring himself to reach for her again.

She'd reject his efforts of comfort. And he honestly couldn't blame her.

He'd made a grave mistake today.

If Caleb didn't make it home, Bri might forgive Ian, but like the rift with her dad, she'd never forget.

And he'd have to live the rest of his life knowing his actions had taken her brother's life away.

"I'll sell it," she said moments later in a catatonic voice.

Ian didn't budge from the couch where he'd been sitting silently, offering his presence. Kate had gone to the trauma center to relieve a nurse who'd hurt her back. Which meant another staff member down and out.

Ian couldn't take much more. Life's walls were closing in, yet it was nothing like what Bri faced. And yet, Caleb was his friend, so he faced it, too.

But this was her brother, her last living relative and the person closest to her on earth, missing in action and presumed a prisoner of war.

No apology or excuse in the world could make up for that.

"Sell something," Bri surprised him by saying.

He knelt nearby but didn't take her hand. Tears dripped to the floor. What had she said? Sell something? "Sell what?"

"The lodge. Cabins. Everything. I'll do anything to bring him back."

"We don't know that he's gone."

A choking sound came out of her throat and Ian could no longer restrain himself. He leaned in and pulled her close.

She didn't pummel his chest, so he held her tight and wished like crazy he were a decent praying man.

"Ian, please pray." She clutched the material of his shirt. He tensed his jaw. Wanted to tell her he couldn't when all of a sudden she began uttering statements. Ian realized she was reading words from the Bible, and turning them to prayers. He closed his eyes and, while he didn't speak himself, he nodded, hoping that might help. At least help her.

Please don't let it be too late to help her brother. The thought had glided in like an eagle over the sapphire lake. Shuffling sounded on the doorstep, then Mitch rushed in. "They got him."

Ian surged to his feet. "The SEALs, or the enemy?"

"SEALs. He's safe. A little banged up, but alive. Headed to a base hospital, courtesy of Pedro."

"Pedro means PJs," Ian explained to Bri. Relief he'd never known befell him like the snowfall outside. He helped Bri to stand, wrapped his arms around her, closed his eyes and for the first time in his life was glad for God giving people a connection of hope to Him through prayer.

She'd needed it. And God had come through.

Caleb and his unit needed it. And God came through.

Ian needed it, but for different reasons. And, apparently, God came through.

Not that Ian deserved it, but God had heard the cry of Bri's heart, had seen her tears. Of that, Ian had no doubt.

"You wouldn't believe it, Caleb. One week after Christmas and there's eighteen inches of snow on the ground. The land and lake is gorgeous." She wouldn't mention the cabins.

Time to let go.

Bri held the phone closer, wishing she could hug Caleb in person. And turn back time.

"Hope it melts and goes away. They can't work safely on a sloped cabin roof with slippery... stuff."

She smiled. "Snow. You're falling asleep again." He sounded so adorable, medicated and groggy. He'd just woken from surgery where they'd removed a bullet from his biceps.

"You hear me?" Caleb's voice grew insistent.

"Don't worry about things here, baby brother. They'll take care of themselves."

"Don't get rid of it, sis."

"What?" She paced until she realized she'd picked up that habit from Ian.

"The retreat. Our lodge. The cabins. I didn't realize until after that bullet knocked me down that I've been selfish."

Bri's throat clogged. She couldn't bear to tell

Caleb that it might be too late for the lodge. She'd made up her mind. Called the loan officer. Left a message and thrown in the towel.

But in turn, Bri was giving everyone their lives back.

"Bri?" Caleb's voice had a distinct supervisory tone.

"I heard you."

"I mean it. You don't realize until your life is in jeopardy what really matters. The lodge, we grew up there. All I thought about lying there waiting for the rescue choppers was the memories. Me. You. Mom. Even Dad. Don't be mad. Not at him. Not at me. Not at Ian. Not at yourself. Life's too short."

The connection crackled. Which was okay, because she couldn't speak, anyway.

But she'd figured out what was most important, too. With the lodge out of the equation, everyone's life would improve. She'd be devastated, but it had to be this way. "You need to go?"

"Prolly."

She smiled. He was drifting off again.

But thankfully, *thankfully,* not forever.

"Knock-knock." Ian's face poked in the cracked door.

Nervousness surrounded him like an aura as he stepped in tentatively. As much as she wanted to be angry with him, she couldn't. Not after what Caleb told her three seconds into their first hour-long conversation this morning. She'd been calling him every other hour on the nose.

"Hey." He eyed her phone. "Caleb okay?"

"Sounds better every time I talk to him."

"That's good. I'm glad, Bri." Deep remorse encompassed his entire being. Guilt. Failure. Shame. She needed to set him free.

"Ian, sit. There's something you should know."

He lowered to her couch but sat on the edge. Tension appeared to grip every pore of his being. He met her gaze without words.

"Caleb didn't know about the fire until today."

Ian's eyebrow furrowed, then his jaw went lax.

"His commander didn't tell him, after all. He thought it best to wait. Ian, you didn't cause the ambush, or cause Caleb not to pay attention. It was just a fluke."

Nothing on earth could measure the discernible relief on his face. "That's good. That's real good." He blew out a long breath and rubbed hands along his thighs.

She wanted to go to him, to eliminate the agony from his tortured eyes. Somehow, during the fire, the snowstorm, the ambush, a bond had formed under duress. Despite Bri's inclination to blame him, Ian had shown up every single day, rain or snow, to hammer away at her cabin.

Whether from a sense of obligation, honor or duty, it didn't matter. He never failed to show. Which was a lot more than she could say for other men in her life. "I can see why you and Caleb have become so close."

He looked up. Angled his face.

"You two are a lot alike." Same moral character. Duty. Honor. Bravery. Hard-work ethic. You name it.

"Listen, I came to apologize."

"No." She got up before he could protest and sat beside him on the couch. "Ian, it's time you stopped seeing and saying everything you think you've done wrong, and start focusing on all the stuff you do right."

He stood, watched snowflakes dance, then cling to the window. "Mesmerizing little things. Aren't they?"

"Miracles, or snowflakes?"

He faced her. Face deadpan. Soft. Sure. "Both."

She nodded, slipped her good arm around his waist and rested her head on his shoulder, giving rather than drawing strength for once.

When she looked up, his eyes were closed, face relaxed. Until he turned, putting them closer than she'd intended. A current of awareness fluttered like an unseen stirring of air. It reached between them, captivating. So soft, so light, barely there.

They simultaneously stepped away. Bri felt a deep emptiness outside the comfort of his nearness.

Voices sounded in her yard. She started outside.

Ian's bulky arm became a barricade. "You don't need to go out in that stuff, Bri. Too risky with your arm."

She peered out the window. Brock and Mitch stood chatting. Each had on coveralls and tool belts. Winter gloves, hats, boots. And it was the first time she could remember when she didn't feel anxiety about people helping. Which was a tragedy, considering the loan officer was set to come assess the land for takeover today.

Should she move back north? No, that meant contending with Eric. She loved Eagle Point, but it would be too painful to stay. Especially if every inch of her childhood was being leveled. At some point, Ian had stepped outside with Mitch and Brock. They pointed toward her cabins that were lakeside. Then toward where the more remote forest cabins stood.

She needed to tell them. Soon.

So they could go back to their lives. Would Ian still let her watch Tia? At least until she figured out where to go from here? Ian pivoted to peer around the perimeter of her property.

Peace shone on his face as he surveyed her land. How would he react when he found out she was probably on the cusp of giving it all up?

Chapter Ten

"Hard to believe the sky's been dumping this for two solid days," Mitch said the next day at the trauma center, after another sleet-related accident filled the last empty trauma bay.

"Unprecedented."

And because of the unusual weather and deep snow, the trauma center crew was stretched to the max.

Something had to give.

Ian faced Mitch. "Dude, we have to hire someone. Or call a rent-a-doc, something. Tia's coming home from Mom's today and I *need* to spend time with her. This is nonnegotiable."

"I'll take care of it." The strain showed on Mitch's face, too, and while he had the stress of planning a wedding, he didn't have a daughter who'd been neglected. "I'll call someone from Refuge to cover for you. Hit the road." Mitch smiled and gave Ian a boot to the hind end. Ian hated feeling as though he was abandoning ship at EPTC, but he was only one person and couldn't be everywhere at once. He eyed his watch. He had a couple hours before his parents and Tia arrived. He called Kate. "You talk to Bri about renting her cabin yet?"

"I will call her soon. I need to make sure my landlord will release me from my lease, but I'm definitely interested."

"Good, because I'm working on the unit you liked best now."

"Sorry I'm not there to help."

"That's fine. Mitch needs you there at the trauma center."

He'd just finished the inside repairs on Bri's third cabin when his parents pulled up. Tia wasn't with them. His mom explained Tia was coming later with Leah, who'd taken her sightseeing in St. Louis at the arch. Ian's sister had taken her for ice cream. Nice. A bouncy child and a matchmaking sister on a sugar high.

Three more vehicles pulled in.

He pivoted. "What on earth?"

"What on earth?" Bri echoed his statement as she stepped onto the deck and joined Ian where he'd walked to greet his mom.

A slew of women and men came bearing food, smiles, work gloves, chain saws and other power tools. "We're here to help," Ian's dad said. Ian's mom shuffled over to hug Bri.

Ian knew Bri was beyond desperate, because relief rather than dread filled her face.

"This is our church's chain-saw ministry," his mom said.

Ian wanted to laugh. "I don't know what scares me more, Mom. A destructive lodge fire followed by two days of unprecedented snowfall…or a bunch of folks bearing chain saws."

The crowd of them laughed good-naturedly. Bri nibbled her lips and looked at Ian with dread. "I need to speak with you right away. Privately, please. Ian, I feel so bad about all these people showing up."

"Bri, I know you have a tough time needing help, but—"

"Ian, that's not it." She drew a heaving breath. "I—I left the loan company office a note, conceding the property."

Shock plumed over Ian's ruddy, handsome face. One that was getting harder each day to look away from. *"What?"*

"Please don't be mad. Try to understand."

"Bri, no. You can't give up."

"I can't go on, Ian. I'm not superhuman."

He gritted his teeth. Paced. Turned back and braced her shoulders with his hands. "No. You can't do this."

"I've already made the decision."

"Under duress." He shook his head slowly. "I won't let you do this. And that loan company is a shark tank, Bri. It's not actually a bank."

"It's basically the same."

Ian felt his anger and sense of justice spike. "No. It's a loan company that preys on people in hardship. Like your mom. Caleb hired an investigator. He uncovered that your mom remortgaged through them due to medical bills. She wasn't thinking clearly. And neither are you."

"So what can I do? I already left a message."

"Did you sign anything?"

"No, but—"

"No buts about it. They are *not* leveling that lodge."

Bri brought her hands up on Ian's. Her face softened. "Ian, I appreciate all you've done. But I don't see any other way."

"Where's your faith, Bri?"

He could tell his words shocked her. Shocked him, too. So maybe he'd retained some of his understanding of God after his divorce.

"Hello?" A voice sounded behind them. The fire chief and another man sauntered up the yard. "Miss Landis, may we talk?"

"Of course." Ian followed her in. The fire chief paying a visit to the home was never a good thing. Right?

Where's your faith?

Ian's own words came back to bite him.

Yeah, yeah, fine. "Did you find out what caused the blaze?" Ian pushed goggles over his snow cap and joined Bri on the couch across from the two somber-faced men.

"Yes. The fire forensics crew determined it was electrical."

"But the electric wasn't aged." Bri stood. Paced.

"No, but it seems because it had been sitting empty for so many months, one of the walls became infested with mice," the chief explained.

Bri's shoulders sank. "Yes, it had. I tried to get rid of them at first, but—but then I recently removed all of the poison and chemicals keeping them away." She'd lowered her voice and darted pensive glances Ian's way, but he still heard.

His gut began to burn. He rotated knots of dread from his shoulders. Leaned in to hear.

"Well, one of those little varmints chewed through the wrong wire. Lit himself up, then set your lodge ablaze."

"A tiny little mouse caught a great big lodge on fire?" Bri blinked disbelievingly.

The other man with the chief cleared his throat. "An electricity spark, actually, but yes, ma'am. I hate to say this, but you might have been better off to leave the poison there until you could get an exterminator."

Bri peered at Ian. "I—I didn't want to cause leukemia in kids, if—if the youth came in after—"

This was his fault. He'd petrified her into removing the chemicals that would have kept the mice away.

Ian went to her side after the men left. "Bri, I'm sorry."

She shook her head. "No, Ian. Don't be. The truth is, I didn't realize those chemicals cause leukemia. I should have known it, but somehow didn't pick that up in child-care classes. If they even taught it. Regardless, I'd rather lose my lodge than have any parent lose their child to cancer."

Ian's jaw clenched. "Once and for all, you will not lose the lodge."

More cars showed up outside. Bri walked to the window. "Oh, dear. I have made an extremely big mess. The whole town just pulled up in my yard. Ian? Do you know what's going on? Why are all these people here?"

Ian couldn't keep the grin from breaking through.

What was happening? Why were all these people here? She went outside, shocked to see more vehicles had arrived. Townspeople and military people dressed in camouflage directed a truck full of roof trusses to her street.

"Good gravy, Ian! You brought in the National Guard?" She palmed the sides of her face.

He chuckled and led her inside. "Caleb called in the Guard. They're guys from his unit who didn't get deployed. I just called a few PJs."

"A few? Ian. This looks like a military base." But she giggled. And couldn't stop. She gasped. "I think the entire town of Eagle Point is here!"

"And most of Refuge," Lem said behind her.

Bri rushed him in a hug. Tears streamed from her eyes. "You helped organize this, didn't you?"

Lem shrugged. "I mighta had a hand in it."

She hugged him. "But what about your Library Read-N-Run fundraiser?"

"That's a month away. Besides, people had to prepay to register for the marathon. That's all said and done. Obviously folks 'round here have it in 'em to give lavishly. To help a neighbor in need. Don't let 'em miss their blessing from God over it, kiddo."

Bri hugged him again. "I love you, Lem." He grinned, seeming well pleased with that. He was Lauren's grandfather, sure, and someone who was very special to Lauren's fiancé, Mitch. Yet Lem was a grandpa figure to everyone. Including Bri now.

Lem approached Ian, who'd grown quiet. "And

you, young man, quit worrying about that trauma center. This year's marathon proceeds are going one hundred percent toward it, and we had an unprecedented level of participation. I think you and my future son-in-law will be pleased with the amount." He gleamed.

"I suppose you don't want me to tell him yet?" Ian eyed Mitch, working on replacing logs with a group of muscular PJs.

"No, it'll be our secret. But I know you got a ton on your mind, especially with that little'n. She's your priority now, not that trauma center."

Lem's words seemed to deeply affect Ian. His parents stood smiling supportively behind him, so apparently it had been weighing on Ian. After listening in on plans, Ian's parents went back to their posts, his mom organizing refreshments for workers and his dad overseeing construction.

"He did that for a living, you know," Ian said of his dad.

The proud look and close bond pricked Bri with a strange feeling: she missed her dad. Deadbeat or not, he was still her father.

Maybe, someday, God would give her courage to go see him.

Bri walked with Ian to meet Kate, who pranced up with a paper. "What's this?" Bri asked.

"My current lease." With that, Kate ripped it

down the middle. "As soon as you get a cabin ready for me, I'll take it."

Ian went to hang with his dad, while Bri walked with Kate to take workers bottled water. "Thank you, Kate."

"Hey, I'm not just doing this to help you. I need to be closer to the trauma center. Twenty minutes is too far away. Living at the cabin means I'd get there in under two minutes."

That made sense. They passed out several cases of water, then rejoined the main fray.

Things were being lifted, sanded, sawed, hammered, nailed, glued, built and caulked all around her. If her mom could only see this, and how it brought the community together like an old-fashioned barn raising, only bigger.

"I wish I could help more," Bri said, raising her arm cast a while later, as a renovation planning team gathered around a brand-new picnic table someone had brought. It looked Amish as far as craftsmanship, just gorgeous.

"You just be the supervisor, telling us what needs to be done," Lem informed. Ian chuckled. Then his face sharpened.

Bri looked up. The loan officer had pulled up and was getting out of his car. The way Ian approached him made her gasp. Lem held her arm. "He's okay. Let him handle it his way."

"Yes, that's what I'm afraid of. You don't know

how mad he looked when I mentioned giving the guy the message he could have the lodge."

"Well, by the looks of things, he's not only leaving in one piece, he'd leaving your lodge alone."

Lauren watched in wonder as Ian spoke a few more words to the red-faced man. Whatever he said sent him back in his car and away. Hopefully for good. Maybe Ian wasn't so dangerous.

He walked up calmly and joined the planning session. Hammering, sawing, laughing, conversation and sounds of massive construction filled the air.

Bri had never heard a sweeter sound.

Lem handed Bri some sketched pages and jotted notes. "Here's the deal. We're gonna have ourselves a citywide New Year's Eve fundraiser bash on Eagle Point's square. Kinda like New York, except not the big, pretty plummeting ball or the trillions of people. I suspect we'll have a few less than that." Lem chuckled. "But still a fairly decent crowd."

"What do you mean by a New Year's Eve fundraiser?"

Ian slid another paper close and brushed her good arm in doing so. She felt disappointed when he moved it away. "All the businesses in town are donating ten percent of their proceeds over the next week to cover this week's construction costs."

Eagle Point's mayor ran a finger down six columns of what had to be three hundred names. "These are business owners and patrons your mom helped out over the last two decades. The night of your fire, they got together to figure out how to help."

Bri gulped. Eyed all the names, gratitude for each one wafting over her. Then gladness over her mom and kindness she'd sewn that Bri was reaping now. Caleb, too, now that he'd figured out the retreat center meant something to him.

The mayor handed her a city meeting minutes. "They proposed fundraising days plus a New Year's Eve shindig on the square. Bands will come to play."

Brock pointed at the vocal lineup. "Ben, my PJ teammate, is killer on guitar. Rowan, our youth pastor, has a set of pipes like Roger Daltrey. A girl in youth group who has a soulful, bluesy voice is going to sing along with a second grungy-voiced girl. Amazing vocalists these kids. They're teenagers from Eagle Point and Refuge who are looking forward to your lodge youth project."

Bri felt overwhelmed with kindness. If all of these people were participating, she realized how important the lodge was to them all. To the community. She looked Ian in the eye. "It seems

Mom's dreams didn't die, after all. They've already come true. All she ever wanted her lodge to do was bring the community together." Bri looked around. "She's done that."

He smiled. Put a hand to the small of her back, a gesture of support, because he knew she'd struggle with receiving the community outpouring of generosity.

But today, that wasn't her only struggle. She struggled to keep her brain from exploding, her skin from zinging and her pulse from hammering every time Ian brushed his hand along hers.

The frightening part was Bri felt more inclined to lean into him than away from him. Things inside her were shifting toward Ian. She was starting to see him in a new way.

And with the brief glances he was sending her way, it was clear he was struggling with the same feelings. Someone cleared their throat behind Bri.

She ripped her gaze off Ian's wide shoulders carrying a log and whirled. Blushed to find his mom smiling behind her. She waved Ian over. "Son, set that naked tree down and come 'ere."

Bri giggled at his mom calling the log a tree. She was thankful for Ian's family coming to help and that Ian's sister had decided to keep Tia in St. Louis for the day so they could see the famed city museum and science center in town.

Thinking this was some sort of family discussion, Bri started to step away. "Whoa, hold on. You stay."

Ian's dad and a few of their friends joined the group.

Ian's mom unfolded a hand-knitted throw blanket that matched the color of the first finished cabin. Also, little matching knitted doilies with country patterns. "You made this?" Bri asked.

She nodded. "Been workin' on it since Christmas. I'll have a few more made in the weeks to come, all for your cabins. But I'll need their individual color schemes."

Every cell in Bri's system felt compelled to protest. Ian's mom, Jenny's, excitement as she stretched out the throw subdued Bri's compulsion. Bri was still smiling when an envelope fell from the blanket as Ian unfurled its ornately scalloped edge.

Everyone grew quiet. Ian watched her carefully. As he might a ticking time bomb. In fact, so did others. Soon, Bri realized that Jenny had waved many of the workers up.

Everyone watched with goofy, expectant grins.

She eyed them in a funny way. "I'm scared to open it now."

Ian shifted. "It's from my family, Lem, Lauren, Mitch and other trauma center staff, plus nearly everyone else in town."

Bri's throat clogged as he peeled the envelope open and slid a check out. She picked it up, couldn't read it because tears blurred her vision. "Oh, that's a lot of zeros." She shook her head. "This is too much. I can't." She shoved it back.

No one would take the check she shoved into the air with frantic, trembling fingers. Ian pressed the check back into her hand, curled her fingers around it and held his hand over hers. Then he squeezed her hand, equally firm and gentle. Like his demeanor. "The lodge benefits Eagle Point. This is your mom's dream." He increased pressure on his hand. "Okay?"

She nodded. Sniffed emotion back. "Okay. When you put it that way, it's easier to accept." But still hard. Bri suddenly wished she could flee. Out of this family who made her miss her own. Out of this situation of needing the help of others. Out of the intoxicating smell of Ian's woodsy cologne. She was about to break down in front of all these happy people.

"Excuse me, I need a minute." Bri slipped away and went inside to the solace of her sunroom, where Tia had learned to swim. Bri realized with an ache in her heart how much she missed Tia.

His mom came in, crossed the room and bent, sidling Bri's face in her hands. "It's a noble thing you're doing, sweet girl, helping my son, my granddaughter, the trauma center and building a haven for teenagers." Now she blinked tears back. As her husband and Ian walked in, Jenny locked gazes with them briefly, before turning back to Bri. "I'll bet you didn't know Ian lost his oldest sister to a drunk driver, did you?"

Bri gulped. Eyed Ian and his misty-eyed family. "I didn't."

"She was my oldest. Got in the car with an intoxicated group of kids. She wasn't drunk but was too scared to speak up or ask to drive. They crashed on a dangerous curve and, well, she's the only one who didn't make it. Ian was ten."

Hard swallows abounded. Hers, too. "What was her name?"

She smiled deeply into Ian's gaze. "Her name was Tiana."

"Tia's named after her?" Bri directed the question at Ian, who was very subdued now.

"Yes." His voice was tight. Hard. Eyebrows pinched.

"I had no idea." Bri rose, took time hugging Ian's parents, then reached behind them and squeezed Ian's hand.

A flicker of emotion shuttered across his face as their hands locked. Ian's fingers twined tightly to hers as she swayed with his parents in a group hug. A commiseration of human hearts who understood the anguish of a family loss. His eyes reached across his parents' backs, to his and Bri's intertwined hands.

Then he met her eyes.

The vulnerable pain swirling deep inside caught her by surprise. He released her hand as though she were live voltage, stepped back and looked the opposite way.

Bri knew his parents hadn't caught it. But she had no doubt what was going through his mind. He'd realized that, unlike his parents, his marriage hadn't stood the test of time. That he no longer had a wife to support, grow old with or help with family endeavors. Every dream of a mate for life, crumbled.

Bri realized with a sickness in her stomach that Ian was crushed with the realization of all he'd lost.

How to give him hope? Would he slip back into full-on brooding? Give himself completely over to it? Or would he open up to the friendship she now desperately wanted to offer?

He'd helped her so much. It was high time he let her help him, too. If nothing more than a shoulder to lean on.

But the stubborn jut to his jaw and the emptiness in his icy aqua-violet eyes, below a hooded, brooding expression, told her that was going to be far easier said than done.

Chapter Eleven

This was not going as planned.

Ian propped his combat boot on his truck runner the next morning and scrubbed his jaw in an effort to rethink everything. Not only was Tia still not adjusting, he was starting to become too drawn to Bri for anyone's good. Especially Tia's.

Ian didn't need anything taking his mind off where his focus should be: rebuilding his relationship with his daughter and taking the best possible care of her.

Unfortunately, Bri's white-silk hair and cornflower-blue eyes were distracting beyond belief. Attraction he could fight, although the battle might drive him insane. This emotional draw to Bri wasn't easy to contend with. Thoughts of her were constantly bombarding his mind.

Hopefully, it just had to do with her confident ability to help Tia. Not to mention she'd had a similar childhood. Perhaps his feelings were merely empathetic. Because nothing else would do.

A tap at his truck door drew his attention. "Hey, Kate."

She jogged up. "Get any rest after the traumas last night?"

"Not really." He kept his voice low, because Bri's cabin sat one hill over. "This the one you picked out?" Ian said when Kate approached the cabin he'd begun applying inside trim to.

"Yeah."

"Sorry you're having to do so much extra work at the trauma center, Kate. You and the rest of the crew. But no one anticipated the center becoming this busy this soon."

"No one minds. You and Mitch gave us secure, well-paying jobs with benefits, both of which are hard for vets to find. I'm surprised you're out here this early." She eyed her watch, then the dark violet sky. It was still oh-dark-thirty. Not yet sunup.

"Tia woke up crying over her mom and asked to come to Bri's early. Bri was awake and happy to see Tia."

Ian ground his knuckles into his sockets to rub out sleep, and the effigy of Bri's eyes, which were *the* blueprint for beauty.

After offering commiseration, Kate said, "I gotta finish my run. See ya later." Kate took off along the lakeside path. Ian walked the woodsy path to the next cabin.

Cicadas seemed the only thing awake at this hour. He slowed his pace to absorb his surroundings. Drew deep whiffs of fresh air. Loved the lush beauty even in winter. The humidity of pre-dawn dew. The deep peace and abiding quiet of morning. Those hours when everything seemed to slumber in unison.

The gentle stir as the sun rose to woo the world awake. Mitch told them on the battlefield that Southern Illinois sunrises and sunsets were splendorous to behold. Not until moving here did Ian fully see. He loved to step out the center's side door to watch the sun's magnificent rise over Eagle Point Lake after long nights. This place were therapeutic.

He could think of nowhere better to raise his little girl than Eagle Point. Although neighboring Refuge was equally family oriented, it wasn't close enough to the trauma center. Ian did love going there to visit Lauren's grandfather, Lem.

Ian approached his truck and hauled more hand tools from the diamond plate industrial box from where he'd been working for a couple hours this morning.

"G'morning," a breathless voice sounded behind him.

He turned to find Bri leaning into a jogger's

stretch with his daughter piggybacked over her shoulders and Mistletoe nestled in her sling. With her broken arm. Ian shook his head. "No wonder Caleb told me to keep an eye on you."

Her hair waged a wrestling match with a lopsided sapphire ponytail band. Flushed cheeks shone through side-swept bangs. Bri's shoes were the type professional runners used. Bri squatted to let Tia slide off her back. Ian appreciated how fit she was.

She'd bundled Tia in gloves and a coat. Today's temps had risen but not enough to melt all the snow. More flakes were forecast.

Ian set his power saw down. "Everything okay?" He really didn't want them in his work space. Too distracting.

"We came to see if you needed anything." She handed Tia a fairy-decorated water bottle, one of two clipped to Bri's trim waist. Tia sipped and dashed under a picnic table to play. Bri faced the lake. "It's beautiful here this time of morning."

His breath almost caught, too. But not because of morning. Her silhouette at sunup would be a portrait painter's dream.

"It's beautiful here anytime. But especially at sunup and sundown." And especially with Bri outlined against the sleepy blue lake. Lovely figure. He looked away, with extreme effort.

She pivoted. "You want to watch the sunrise with me?"

Because he very much *did* want to, he put his best scowl forward. "No. As you can see, I have work to do."

Her smile faded. "I'll come back with Tia and help with cleanup as soon as we take Mistletoe back for his nap in a bit."

He grunted. "I didn't say you had to help. I can manage this part by myself. Others are coming later, too."

Her forehead dipped in such a way she resembled a rodeo bull ruminating a horns-first charge. "I can help."

"I'd rather you didn't."

"It's *my* cabin." Her good hand jammed her hip. Okay. So she could be as stubborn as him. Ian swiveled away. He pulled a broken window screen. It stuck.

Bri, emitting cute little scoffing noises, tromped to help but must've realized she couldn't with one arm. She walked over to where Tia played fort under a picnic table with Mistletoe. Bri smiled at the pair, then refaced the lake.

Eyes flitting his way, her face tensed. Was she resisting the urge to whack him? Or simply struggling with her inability to help work on cabins? She intently watched the sky turn vivid colors, her face transforming under a bright orange-and-baby-blue-streaked sunrise. Ian tried not to notice how beautiful she was. He forced himself not to engage her in conversation, either.

Bri suddenly stomped close. "Why are you in such a sour mood?"

Tia's mom promised her she'd call last night and didn't.

Ian had been in a foul mood since. Not to Tia. She wouldn't have noticed, anyway. She'd ignored him like a piece of broccoli in an enemy's tooth. Not to mention the battle over real broccoli last night. Not even melted cheese enticed Tia to eat the vegetables she pushed away like a plate of worms.

She'd thrown in Ian's face that her mom never made her eat broccoli. The nice dinner he'd planned? Turned to total disaster in front of an entire ritzy restaurant because of a phone call that never happened. Tia had convinced herself it was Ian's fault.

Then somehow, he did, too.

"Ian? Is everything okay?" Bri drew near. Too close. He almost softened to unload everything on her. He made a colossal effort to keep his mouth—and heart—shut.

After an eternal moment, she stepped gingerly back. "Okay, well…I'm here if you need to talk."

Silence. For the longest, most agonizing seconds, he didn't budge. Then just when he thought the emotional coast was clear, she moved like an automatic bullet to stand behind him. So close, her presence felt like warm whispers against his back. He kept his head down and his spine to her, because if he saw the kindness in her face, he'd cave.

After long, tense moments, he felt her presence wane again.

He fought against the urgency to reach out, to accept the friendship she offered. If divorce hadn't sufficiently convinced him that would be the second stupidest move he could ever make, he might've done so. But no. Too risky.

He'd rather forfeit friendship than prosper pain.

And the romance his mom kept hinting at? Not even on his radar. It had taken too big a bite out of his heart once to make him want to try again.

With Bri out of sight, his head cleared enough to focus on sawing damaged areas of structure without cutting himself.

After a while, Bri and Tia brought out two cups of coffee. The one she drank out of was dainty and had a chip in it. In fact, she drank out of that one every time he'd seen her.

"It was Mom's favorite," she said when she caught him staring at it. He nodded, resisting the urge to chat. When she talked, he became mesmerized.

"Is black coffee okay?"

"I prefer cream and sugar," he said stiffly.

She smirked. "I'm more than happy to oblige."

"What's that mean?" And why was she snickering?

She whirled gracefully. "Maybe the sugar will sweeten you up." She grinned when she said it.

He returned to ripping off old wood with fervor. Irritation for not knowing how to handle his emotions accosted him. Feeling seemed too raw and risky right now. He didn't want to feel anything. Period.

Well, except the ends of her silky hair that tumbled down her back as she released her ponytail just now.

That's it. Ian stepped onto another portion of scaffolding that would put her completely out of view.

A yip sounded nearby. Bri though, not the dog. Tia giggled as Mistletoe chewed the tendon on the back of Bri's ankle. Ian watched the pup's antics and bit back a grin. He refused to have fun today. Fun created a bond he couldn't deal with. Not with the argument with Tia's mom last night fresh on his mind. Ava refused to give reasons or apologize for not calling Tia as promised. And she'd declined to speak to Tia when he called.

Women broke promises. They didn't honor commitments.

He studied Bri and didn't give himself the opportunity to consider otherwise. To do so would cheat Tia out of the full concentration of his heart. Shame on him for noticing anything appealing about Bri. But even wearing a camouflage sweatshirt, she was beautiful.

The rest of the day, Ian put his full effort into renovating the cabin…and ignoring this ridiculous attraction to Bri.

The next morning, Bri watched Ian step into the cabin. Tia sat stiffly in his arms with red, blotchy eyes. Clearly, there had been a tantrum this morning.

Ian set her down in Bri's front room and tried to help her off with her coat. Tia jerked away. Ian's jaw clenched. He eyed his watch. "I needed to check a patient two minutes ago."

Bri swarmed in. "Go. I'll take over."

"Thanks. Bye, Tia. See you in a bit. Love you."

Her answer was a scowl. Until he was out of sight, at which time she ran to the window with wistful, sorry eyes. Proving to Bri that Tia loved him, after all.

A few hours later, Tia leaped from their puzzle, and gasped. "It's snowing again! Can we play in it? And take Mistletoe?"

"For a bit." Bri bundled Tia in gloves, hat and her coat.

They played in the snow until Ian pulled up

in his truck. He approached Tia, who pointed to Mistletoe.

"The puppy doesn't like snow. It sticks to his feet and his belly and he tries to eat it," Tia said matter-of-factly to her dad. So whatever rift they'd had this morning must've waned.

Mistletoe's tail wriggled and he tried to run toward Ian, who looked regretful for not engaging the pup. To Bri's, and Tia's, delight, Ian scooped up the pup. "If this keeps up, we'll need to get you a doggie snowsuit, little guy." Ian scratched the dog behind the ears, then snuggled him in his jacket so only his face poked out the top of Ian's coat zipper.

Bri grabbed her phone, because this picture was too cute to miss. "That is adorable, Ian." She went to pet the dog and caught whiffs of Ian's cologne. Her knuckles accidentally brushed his chest, causing his breathing rhythm to hitch.

He broke the connection by stepping back. But space didn't dissipate warmth wafting off his tanned neck that reminded her of a cozy fireplace. Or dampen the image of a chest developed by hard work and disciplined exercise. And most certainly didn't wipe the memory of the flicker of awareness in his eyes.

"I came bearing good news this time." He smiled wryly. "Mitch hired a new anesthesiologist." He knelt in front of Tia. "Which means I'll be taking more time off to spend with you."

Tia's eyes brightened, then were beset by a scowl. "But I'm still mad at you about Mommy."

What did that mean? Bri wondered.

Ian didn't comment. "Would you like to meet the new doctor? She was hired today, and I start training her tomorrow. She's from very far away, so we should make her feel welcome."

"Can we take her cookies, Miss Bri?"

Bri felt a ripple of…something. Couldn't be jealousy, right? She had not staked a claim on Ian. Bri groaned inwardly. "I'll get the cookies." She dashed in. When she returned, Tia and Ian put twig arms in the snowmen she and Tia had built. Bri smiled.

Ian stood on her approach. "Ready?" They walked together across the lot. Ian asked Tia for the third time if she wanted him to carry her. She pulled away sharply when he tried to take her hand or pick her up, proving Tia was still upset over something, probably Ava. Bri's heart broke for them.

With Tia surging a few steps ahead, Bri lagged behind to squeeze Ian's arm to infuse strength. It backfired, because what she felt under his shirt was a pile of muscles that made her knees weak. *Lord, I need to get out more and date.* Who was she kidding? She barely had time to daydream, much less make one come true.

"So, this new doctor...where's she from exactly?"

"Alaska. Her brother's in the coast guard there." Ian scratched his jaw as if determining how much to say. "Apparently she's just endured the loss of her marriage and another tragedy. I'm not sure if she's a recent widow or divorcée or what. She's young, though, for a doctor." Ian faced Bri with a meaningful look. "It seems I have you to thank for bringing her here."

"Me? Why? How?"

"Whatever she went through caused her to need to leave her area. That's the idea Mitch got while interviewing her. She'd been looking for a place far from home and the hardship she endured there. She answered a physician recruiter ad for our trauma center. She researched us, then Eagle Point's history. She's been accessing the town news feed."

"You mean the *Four Guys, a Dog and a Blog* feed?"

"Yes. When she read about how the town came together to save your lodge and other things, she booked the next flight out."

"Not even knowing if Mitch would hire her?"

"She said regardless of whether she got a job at EPTC, she'd commute as far as St. Louis if she had to. She felt drawn to the area, especially since Refuge claims to live up to its name and Eagle Point is a haven of the same magnitude."

Bri didn't like the little niggles of sourness hitting her with Ian's excitement. Good grief. No way was she jealous.

Not until she stepped inside the nurses' station and saw how movie-star glamorous the new anesthesiologist was.

And Ian would be training her and working with her. Ugh.

Bri needed to get a grip. It wasn't as if she had feelings for Ian or anything. So why this sense of panic?

Mitch ushered the sophisticated doctor toward them. "This is Bri and Tia, Ian's daughter. Meet Dr. Lockwood."

"Please, call me Clara." The stunning woman approached. Held Bri's gaze, then Tia's as she gracefully knelt. "Are those for me?"

Tia pressed the cookies in the doctor's hand. "Yes, ma'am."

The beautiful doctor smiled fondly at Ian. Too fondly. "Your dad's been telling me all about you and what a good little baker you are. Thank you very much for the cookies." She took a bite. "They're the best I've ever tasted."

Bri grit her teeth. Caught Kate watching her over the desk. Bri averted her gaze. When Bri looked back up, Ian was watching her, too. Bri snapped herself out of it and put on a happy face. She reached out her hand. "I'm Bri. Welcome to Eagle Point."

The doctor's kind smile and warm handshake made Bri feel bad about the snarky thoughts flying through her head.

"Is that your little girl?" Tia brushed fingers along a silver locket pin resting over the doctor's heart.

No way did Bri miss the pain flashing across the astute doctor's eyes. She clutched the locket and knelt in front of Tia. "Yes." Her voice all but fractured.

Ian's gaze sharpened, as did Kate's and Mitch's.

"Can I play with her?"

The doctor brushed trembling fingers over Tia's cheek and struggled to speak for a moment. "I sure wish you could." Convulsive swallows shone in her throat. "But, she went to go live in heaven a couple of months ago." The doctor smiled kindly, but tears swam in her eyes. Bri found herself tearing up, too.

The dispatch alarm toned an incoming trauma. The new doctor's face livened with relief. She stepped back and cast embarrassed, apologetic glances all around. The crew offered graceful nods and compassionate, reassuring looks, clearly all hearts going out to her. Though everyone undoubtedly wondered, no one asked about the recent trauma that took her daughter's life. Dr. Lockhart moved next to Ian as though he were a harbor.

Lauren brought a note to the doctors. "Ambulance two minutes out." Ian, somber, eyed the note, then Bri.

Bri picked up Tia. "We should go before that comes in."

Ian nodded, studying her like a hawk. Bri waved nonchalantly and avoided Kate, who was trying to intercept her on the way out. This was nonsense. She felt *nothing* for Ian. So why did the new doctor being so pretty make her feel so threatened?

She'd let herself get too close to Ian. Dependent. To care and be cared for. She'd joined their tight-knit fray of friendship. That's all this was. Yet why didn't Bri feel threatened by Kate in that case? Because Kate never looked at Ian like the lady doctor had.

Bri shook off the stupid thought. "Tia, this way."

Halfway across the lot, she caught Tia eyeing her sling. "I been wondering, what happened to your arm?"

"I fell off a ladder and broke it. Your dad helped me."

Tia gasped. "He helped you fall and break it?"

Bri laughed. "No, silly goose. I broke it all on my own. He helped me afterward. I'm very thankful he was close by."

Tia glanced back to the center, where an ambulance pulled in. "He helps lotsa people. It's why he went away for a very long time in the war." Tia looked thoughtful yet downtrodden, as if she wanted to run back and hug him like there was no tomorrow. But there was, thanks to God and answered prayer.

"He tells me he's glad to be back. You're the best part of his life now." Bri took Tia to check on Mistletoe snoozing in his kennel with a new blanket Bri suspected Ian had gotten him.

"Why wasn't I the best part before?" Tia's face shuttered.

Bri didn't know what to say to that. Ian was right. Tia had extraordinary wisdom, reasoning and vocabulary beyond her years and therefore was harder to deal with than most kids her age.

"What happened to the little girl?" Tia eyed EPTC as they climbed the steps to Bri's cabin decks.

"I'm not sure. I feel terrible for her, though, don't you?"

Tia nodded, somber. "Yes. I'm sad about me, too. Boom isn't as fun as a real friend."

Bri hugged her shoulders. "Me and your dad will work on finding friends for you." Tia's eyes lit up, so Bri amended, "Which is to say, I'll talk with your dad about finding you some playmates."

Walking into the kitchen, Bri gathered Jonah's fish food. Since it would be a while before Mistletoe reached countertops, they decided it was safe to keep him at Bri's for ease of feeding and because Ian's hours were unpredictable.

At least, they were before a pretty Alaska doctor came.

Bri scowled at herself and her silly insecurities, especially in light of Dr. Lockhart's horrific loss.

Tia ran up when she saw the fish food. "Can I do it?"

"Yes, but only as much as I showed you. Overfeeding Jonah can hurt him." Bri observed the fantailed fuchsia creature.

Tia sprinkled the pinch as Bri had shown her. Tia sighed. "I didn't deserve the fishy. Or my new dolly." Tia's chin and shoulders drooped. "Santa needs new glasses. I was very bad."

Bri leaned elbows on the counter. "Why do you say that?"

"I was mean to Da—him." She jabbed a finger toward the trauma center. Bri knew she meant Ian. "He said I'd see Mommy on Christmas and I didn't. I was very mad and messed up my room. Then Grandma told me it was Mommy's fault."

Hurray for Ian's mother. Bri wiped Tia's tears. "And you feel bad for blaming him?"

Tia nodded. Finger in her mouth, she dipped her head.

Bri wrapped her arms around her and held her close. "Tia, he understands. He's hurting, too, mostly for you."

Tia quivered. "He might get mad enough to leave."

"No. That will never happen. He loves you despite what you do. Always remember that, okay?"

Tia's expression relaxed, but not the writhing of her hands.

Bri picked one of the books she'd given Tia for Christmas that Tia wanted to leave here. "Want to read this one?"

After reading books, Tia asked to watch a movie.

Bri picked out a *Cinderella* DVD. "How about this one?"

Tia sifted through the stack. "That one looks good, but I was hoping for *Tinker Bell*. She's a fairy, you know."

"So I've heard. It doesn't look like she's here." Bri looked again through the animated movies Ian had brought to be sure. "I'll mention to your dad about *Tinker Bell*."

"No!" Tia clutched Bri's good arm. "Please don't ask him."

Bri turned at Tia's fearful tone. "He won't get angry at you asking for something."

"Mama does. Did. She got very mad. So I never asked."

Bri knelt. She had to be careful with her words. The fact that Tia was starting to speak of her mother in the past tense spoke volumes. "Would you like me to ask your dad for you?"

"Will he get mad?"

"I really don't think he will."

Bri thought she heard her door open and close. Probably Kate. She was supposed to drop another arm bandage by for Bri.

"I had Tinker Bell slippers at home." Tears began to roll down Tia's face. "At my mom's home. Not at Ian's."

Bri wondered why Tia had to leave her mom's so fast she hadn't gotten to take all her stuff. She'd ask Ian for information later.

"He's your dad, Tia." *Please give him a chance.* "It's disrespectful not to call him that, even when you feel so mad you don't want to."

"But I do want to," Tia's lips said, but her eyes whispered she just couldn't. Not yet. Wow. Bri did not expect that response or the barrage of Tia's conflicted tears that followed.

Bri's heart twisted in empathy. As she looked into the pain-speckled eyes of the cutest little girl this side of the Mississippi, whose heart had become too hollowed to hope, Bri suddenly felt way in over her head as she hugged Tia gently.

Way in over her heart, too.

Lord, I don't know what to say or do.

This was going to be far more difficult, and heart-wrenching, than Bri imagined.

When she looked up in the doorway and locked gazes with Ian's remarkably kind and handsome eyes above Tia's head, she knew falling for him was going to be easier than she imagined, too.

"Tia, you know how we're rebuilding the lodge? God puts broken things and people back together, too."

Ian caught it as well as Tia, because he turned his cheek slowly, attention going retro on her words. He stared at Bri for a full minute, then, "Doing okay, T-ia?"

No missing it. Ian's voice changed on his daughter's name. A hitch in cadence. A hairline fracture in tone. His fingers had also fluttered over his heart at her mention. He turned to go.

The truth hit Bri like a hurricane: rudeness wasn't Ian's prime problem.

He was hurting for his daughter.

His curtness and silence were symptoms. She was beginning to understand how he was wired. Beginning to care too much.

Lord, I took this on, and You know how hard

it is for me to ask for help. I'm in over my head, and unless I'm imagining things, I'm about to be in over my heart. Please help me.

Chapter Twelve

Ian's phone rang the next morning. Lem's farm-tanned face and huge grin lit the screen. Ian smiled, too. "Hey, Lem."

"Howdy, partner," Lem said in his Southern Illinois twang. "I'm calling to remind you my chili cook-off's today instead of Saturday because of the New Year's Eve shindig. It'd mean a lot to me if you and your little'n would come join the fun today."

Ian considered the progress they'd made on cabins. Thought about how Lem had spearheaded a great portion of the help. "We'd love to. I'll get Tia ready and head over."

"Say, bring that babysitter of yours, too. She hasn't had the pleasure of tasting my chili yet, and I don't want Mitch to beat me to her."

Ian laughed at the friendly war Lem and Mitch waged over who could make the best chili. Hence the chili cook-off.

"I'll see if she'll accompany us." Ian felt strange calling Bri, but really, she needed a day out of the house, too.

"Hello?" she answered in a still-groggy voice.

Ian was stricken with how feeble she'd looked the day she'd met Dr. Lockhart, who, admittedly, had clung to Ian like Velcro. He knew it merely stemmed from a professional bond they shared over practicing in the same career field. Why had Bri looked so apprehensive?

Ian cleared his throat. "Hey, we're headed to Lem's today and wondered if you'd want to ride along. Kate and Lauren will be there, too," he tacked on, so it wouldn't seem like a date or anything.

Ian loosened the neck of his shirt, which suddenly felt tight.

"Mmm, sure. That sounds fun. Mitch has been asking me to try his chili, anyway."

"Oh, no. You have to try Lem's first. Or Lem's likely to drag me across his cornfield by my ear, like he used to do with Mitch when he was younger and wreaking havoc in Lem's fields."

Bri giggled. "Yes, Sarge. I'll be ready in ten minutes."

And she was. Bri wore jeans, rodeo cowgirl boots with suede eagles on them and a chambray top that had glitter strands woven in its plaid. Tia reached out and brushed her hand along it when Bri leaned in to put a wool blanket in the seat. "Ooh! Pretty! Pink and purple and shiny."

Bri ruffled Tia's hair. "I wore it just for you."

"Sit with me!" Tia patted the backseat. Bri climbed up.

Ian drove on the road leading from Eagle Point to Refuge where Lem's farm was, confounded more each mile as to why it had disappointed him when Bri hadn't sat in the front.

At Lem's, the chili cooking was in full swing, with Mitch and Lem ribbing each other. The married PJs' kids immediately took to Tia and included her in their games and antics. "We should've brought Mistletoe," Bri said, watching them fondly.

"Next time," Ian promised, then approached Lauren, who was giving tractor rides. Ian booted Lauren off, then faced Bri. "Want to see Lem's place?"

"Sure." Ian helped her up, then fired it up. Kate and the PJs' wives oversaw the kids. Ian took Bri for a rickety spin around Lem's property. She giggled every time he went over ruts. Ian didn't want to admit how much fun he was having. On the trail, Ian pointed out wildlife that didn't spook or run at their approach. River otter, deer, rabbits and a turkey.

Twenty minutes into the ride, Bri pointed to a turtle upside down in the road. "Ian, look! Poor little thing."

"First off, he's not little." Ian shut the tractor off and lifted Bri down, reveling in how right she felt that brief instant in his arms. "Second…" Ian blanked. Her proximity didn't help matters.

Bri blinked wide at Ian. He realized he still held her around the waist. "Sorry," he muttered, yet didn't actually feel one bit sorry. Bri clutched his arm as he approached the turtle.

He stepped close enough to see what kind it was. Bri leaned out. His arm halted her back. "Hold up, Bri. He's a snapper." Ian took a stick and tried to push him off the road. The turtle hissed and clawed but only moved in a circle. He was too heavy for the stick. And madder than all get-out.

"My word, he's a temperamental thing."

"He'll hurt you like crazy if he bites you, so stay back."

"Isn't that just like us? Our world flips upside down, then we lash out at the one trying to set us right?" Bri eyed Ian pointedly.

She had a point. But he was on a mission. He was getting the stubborn thing to safety despite its cantankerous nature.

"If I can get him to the ditch, I can turn him right side up." Ian nudged the turtle with his boot, but the shell simply spun. The turtle hissed. Ian tried again. No go.

Finally, Ian grabbed the tail end of the shell and hefted the hissing creature toward the ditch. "Stand way back," Ian hollered, then, flipping the turtle over, set it down quickly and leaped away like an antelope.

"Ian!" Bri screeched, then burst out in a run and hysterical laughter as the angry snapper shot forward and went after Ian.

"They're faster and heavier than they look." He leaped onto the tractor, where she'd scrambled. The turtle crawled slow and stout toward them. He came to a stop below their feet and proceeded to hiss and stare them down. "Don't step down, whatever you do." Now Ian's voice cracked with laughter, too. It'd been a long time since he'd laughed this freely. It felt good. Liberating.

Bri's head dipped, shoulders quaked with snickers. "Sorry, Ian, it's just if you could've have seen your face when he came out of that ditch after you." Her words gave way to giggles.

Ian chuckled, too. The turtle continued to hiss and stalk.

Bri shifted uncomfortably, making Ian realize

she hung on one-handed. This wouldn't do. He hoisted her up into the seat.

"What are we going to do?" she said between snickers.

"Hey, far as I'm concerned, that was a trap." Ian jabbed a finger at the turtle. "He can get his grumpy self off the road this time." Ian lifted up his pant leg, showing Bri where the turtle had snipped a hole in his jeans. Ian had ripped the material free, jerking and dragging the turtle with him.

Bri gasped. "I didn't realize they were so mean."

Ian made a scoffing sound but eyed her adoringly. "Yeah, *poor thing,* my foot." He shook his head and pulled himself up.

Her face deadpanned. "Ian, you can't just leave him there."

"Me? Seriously? After he hissed and snapped like that, you want me to risk life and limb to help him?"

Her eyes turned a lot like Mistletoe's. Irresistible. He sighed. But climbed over the other side of the tractor and used the stick to lure the turtle far enough off the road he'd be safe. The turtle snapped at the branch all the way to the forest, whipping around every so often to run at Ian's dancing feet. Bri's melodious voice rang, face flushed from laughing.

Ian climbed back on the tractor and peered into the forest, whose majestically hued leaves were scattered among foliage now camouflaging the snapper. Ian realized with wonder that for the first time in a long time, he felt relaxed, stress-free and calm, despite having been chased by one of the biggest, meanest, fastest turtles he'd ever seen.

He started the tractor, still grinning. "Tia tells me all the time how fun you are to be with, Bri. I see what she means."

Bri's smile could reverse a sunset. Ian's sense of well-being increased as she snuggled into him a tiny bit more than before. "Cold?" he asked.

She shook her head and elevated her arm on his leg as if they were the best of friends. Maybe these days they were.

Comfortable. Safe. Constant. That's what she felt like.

And this time, it had absolutely nothing to do with her being the babysitter. "Bri, you make me believe it's possible to enjoy life again."

She shifted in the seat to peer at him. "It's always possible, Ian. You'll see." My goodness, her sweet smile and stunner eyes almost made him run Lem's tractor into a tree. That would be bad.

Meanwhile, did Bri have any idea what she was walking into?

"Fair warning. Everybody is probably all wondering where we went," Ian warned. "And why we were gone so long."

Bri's cheeks tinged. "Surely they'll believe us and not tease us or come to the wrong conclusion."

Ian burst out laughing. "You don't know them very well."

Bri gasped. "What will the children think?"

Ian slowed the tractor and turned around, his eyes with a teasing glint. "They'll think I stopped and gave you a kiss."

Her eyes widened. She smacked his shoulder. Ian's ears went ablaze when he blurted that.

"Sorry. That was probably inappropriate."

Bri grew very quiet. Fidgety, too. He hadn't meant to embarrass her. But apologizing over his poor choice in subject matter would only bring it up again. Best not to.

The rest of the trip was a bit more subdued, yet Ian still didn't want his time with Bri to end. Was he veering into dangerous waters? He really wasn't sure.

"Me next, me next!" Tia exclaimed when Ian parked in Lem's yard. Bri scrambled off and helped Tia into the front. He ignored the smirks and direct stares from the PJs and his trauma crew. Even Lem had an ornery glint in his eyes.

Great. The matchmakers were in full swing,

and Lem was their unswerving ringleader. "Tia, want to go see bunnies?"

"Yay!"

Mitch helped her up. Ian wrapped a protective arm around her and off they went.

Tia giggled and squealed more than Bri had. Ian smiled. "Who knew one could have so much fun on a tractor?"

"Lookie!" Tia said as they pulled back into Lem's yard.

"Looks like they're getting ready for a hay-ride." Ian indicated the long trailer filled with hay bales.

Ian helped Tia off and settled her next to Bri at the tables. Bri smiled up at him, nearly making him trip. He couldn't seem to take his eyes off her.

And Kate wouldn't stop snickering behind her hand. Ian gave her a narrowed gaze and shook his head. Attraction or not, Ian couldn't feed this. A wistfulness went through him that made him wish he could. If only he'd met Bri at a different time in life.

She caught his gaze. He looked away. Went to help Mitch hook up the flatbed trailers to the tractors. While everyone was loading between the two, Ian helped Bri up, then settled himself and Tia next to her. But not too close.

Kate swept in and scooped Tia from Ian's

arms. "This little one's coming with me." Kate put Tia on her shoulders and galloped to the other trailer. Tia giggled all the way.

"Excuse me," Bri said beside him as PJs and their wives crammed in so tight it forced Ian and Bri to scoot together. Bri's eyes widened. Ian shot them all a lethal look. "What's wrong with the other side of the trailer?"

There were plenty of seats over there. Yet Bri didn't move and, admittedly, Ian didn't, either. It was just because she'd brought her wool blanket and hayrides this time of year could get chilly, he told himself.

Nothing more.

"Cold?" Ian asked Bri a half hour later.

She shivered. "A little." But she'd ended up sending her blanket to the trailer that had the most kids. "I didn't realize there would be a hayride or I would have brought a heavier coat." Her teeth chattered, causing her to be embarrassed.

Ian eyed the couples around him and how the men had arms draped around the women. All except Brock, huddled under two hoodies and sleeping like a newborn.

"He's used to being in extreme elements," Ian said.

Bri shook her head. "Unbelievable."

Ian scooted closer to her and draped his arm

around her. "Body heat," he explained. Then winced, probably hoping that hadn't come out wrong. Bri enjoyed the warmth and snuggled under the crook of his shoulder.

Pretty soon she rested her head on his arm and he didn't tense or squirm. She peered up through her lashes to find him fighting back a grin. Bri was just glad for the warmth. Period. It just so happened that her heater was a human heartthrob. That explained why her senses were on hyperalert being so near to him.

Ian leaned against her, too, after a while longer, adding to Bri's warm feeling. He'd let her lean long enough, and finally, he was leaning back. "Thanks, Ian." It came out a murmur, causing him to peer down at her.

"It feels nice to just kick back and relax and enjoy a full moon on a nice winter night with friends." Two screech owls let it rip, causing Bri to slam against Ian. He peered down at her and smiled. Then drew her closer. "Don't worry. I'll protect you from those vicious old owls." His arm around her felt very much like a hug, and caused curious glances to drift their way. Now people would assume for sure. *But I'm just the babysitter.*

How many times was she going to have to repeat that phrase over the next three days now?

Once back at Lem's house, which was actually

an elaborate houseboat on dry land surrounded by fields and wildlife, Tia rushed up with Lauren. "Daddy! The kids invited me to a lock-in. Can I go, please?"

The other group of kids Tia's age chorused her *pleases*. Lauren approached Ian. "We have plenty of room for her and plenty of adults to watch them. We have fun activities planned."

"Where's this?" Ian asked, scratching his temple.

"At Refuge Community Church, in the children's church section. We have an extra sleeping bag she can use. Ben's little girl lives on the way and has clean pajamas Tia can wear."

Bri knew Ben as the Asian-American PJ who'd sung and strummed silly songs on his guitar for the kids while the adults sat near Lem's campfire looking on and clapping.

"Please?" Tia stood on tippy-toes and clasped her hands.

Ian studied her. His face had literally melted when she'd called him Daddy. Tia probably wasn't even aware she had, which made Bri smile because it meant deep down, Daddy was how she thought of him.

"I suppose, since you'll be well supervised, you may go."

Tia and the other children erupted in cheers. Ian smiled.

"Nice to see her happy," Bri said on the way to Ian's car.

The peaceful look fled his face. The muscle rippled in his jaw. She scrambled in front of him. "Ian, I'm so sorry. I didn't mean she's not happy other times, like with you."

He shrugged. Raised his arm as if to be free of her hand.

"I'm sorry."

He shook his head. Flickered a glance her way. "Not you. You just stated the obvious."

"Ian, for what it's worth, I think Tia realizes you're a good dad and that you love her. But right now, she's a lot like that turtle, out of her element and lashing out, unable to understand situations beyond her comprehension." What little girl could fathom a mother's abandonment? Bri was twenty-six years old and still struggling with her father's choices. "Tia confessed to being lonely for friends. I told her I'd mention it."

A cold chill gripped Bri's spine when she thought of her dad being all alone with no one. How would she even know him if she never went to see him? Bri gritted her teeth against the thought. Seeing her dad was the last thing she wanted.

Or so she thought. Somehow the thought of her own dad dying alone and never being forgiven gave her a dismal outlook.

"You okay?" Ian peered down at her, his concern evident.

"Mmm-hmm. Peachy."

"Liar." His eyes remained kind and his voice tender when he whispered it. Scary that he was getting to know her so well.

Because his eyes were curiously magnetic, she had to face another way. She indicated the tractor, which had logged many miles today. "That was fun, Ian. Thank you for inviting me."

The chaperones gathered children to leave. Tia surprised them by running up and hugging Ian. "Goodbye. Thank you."

Ian's smile could power the universe. "Have a good time."

Since other goodbyes were being said, Bri gathered her wool blanket and bid Lem and the others good-night. She felt stares and sensed curiosity, but because people were being respectful and honest about it, she wasn't bothered by it.

She could tell Ian was seriously embarrassed, though. She could tell he'd gotten hammered with questions by his guy friends. She snickered. He deserved all the teasing he got, since he'd embarrassed her with that kiss statement.

Boy, had that surprised her. What had made him say it?

No way had he been thinking about kissing her. Most likely he'd been telling the truth. Still, it had been an awkward yet catalytic moment. Because in truth, the beautiful landscape of Lem's property and the canopy of trees under a romantic silver moon would've been a prime setting for a kiss. For a couple who liked each other *that* way.

Yet for a second, Bri experienced disappointment.

Once at the vehicles, Ian opened his truck door and helped her in. "How's your arm?"

"It's okay. Little jarred from the hayride and road ruts."

He went to his side, and she was overwhelmed with how his muscles flexed when he swung himself up into the truck. She veered her eyes away. Ian seemed nervous, his legs fidgety over the few miles between Refuge and Eagle Point.

The closer he got, the slower he drove. He seemed in deep thought, as if he had something to say. At least he wasn't brooding. Once on Lakeview, he repositioned again, this time more pronounced. "So, uh, Bri. I was wondering, would you wanna hang out a little longer? Watch some TV?"

Was he asking her on a date? Nah. Probably just sick of watching cartoons. "How about a family friendly marathon?"

He grinned. "Sounds perfect."

No, perfect was his subsequent boyish grin. "Wanna watch it at your house or mine?"

"Mistletoe's at my house and so is Jonah."

"Didn't want you to think you aren't welcome at my place."

She studied him. "I break in on a regular basis, don't I?" To get Tia clean clothes and switch out storybooks, but still.

"True." He smirked. "I'll get the dog," Ian said as they entered her cabin. Bri smiled when she heard the tender playful way Ian interacted with the pup. Nowhere in sight was the beastly guy who drove her crazy sometimes. Bri fed Jonah, who flipped around in the tank in an apparent show of hunger.

Just as Bri put the movie on, Ian's cell rang. He tossed his head back and groaned. Disappointment hit her too at the thought he'd have to leave.

He eyed his phone, then answered. "Hey, Mitch." Ian stood and peered out her window to the trauma center. "What's up?" He stilled, angling his head toward her briefly. "I'm, well, uh, I'm at Bri's."

She pulled her feet onto the couch and observed Ian squirm. She knew full well he wasn't ashamed of her. Just not wanting to have to face the razzing.

"Yeah, I can do that. Not a prob." His shoulders slumped. "Nah, there's no need for you to drive all the way out here. We were just hanging out, about to watch some T.V. Sure. Bye."

After the call ended, Ian approached slowly.

Bri uncurled her feet. Stood. "You have to leave?"

He cradled his phone and tilted his head, peering at her as if determining whether she'd be upset. "'Fraid so."

Now her shoulders slumped. His gaze swept to her face, so she covered her disappointment by rotating her shoulder, pretending stiffness. "I understand. I'll walk you to the door." She headed there, wanting out from under the intent way he was looking at her.

At the door, he didn't slip out but leaned in. "Do you, Bri?"

She raised her chin, only now realizing she'd stared dismally at the floor. "Of course. Mitch probably needs you to go check on a patient or something. I get it."

Face tilting the opposite way, he reached his hand as if to cup her face, then let his fingers fall.

She felt frozen to the spot. The air turned heavy around them, his eyes sedate as they roved over her face. "Just making sure you understand I'm not thrilled about having to leave."

She met his eyes. Saw the same curious wonder in them that she felt swirling inside. "Me, too."

Ian held the doorknob, looking extremely conflicted. Then extremely interested in her mouth.

His gaze held there, then jetted to her eyes. Then he knuckled her door's wood panel, sighed heavily and slipped out.

Whoa.

Had she not known better, she might have concluded he'd been contemplating a good-night kiss. But that would mean they were more than just friends.

She watched him go as he cast meaningful glances over his shoulder all the way to his truck.

Friendship felt safe. His brooding she could handle. This new sense of wonder? Not so much.

Chapter Thirteen

He had to be losing his ever-loving mind.

Ian ground his teeth and slammed the snooze on his alarm clock again in a state of total exhaustion. He'd had to go pick up Tia from the lock-in because she couldn't stop crying for him. A plus—yet then he'd tossed and turned all night thinking about Bri. Then once sleep did come, he'd dreamt about her, her pretty eyes, soft voice, sweet laugh.

He stretched, rubbed eyes that were scratchy and unwilling to open then stumbled down the hall to wake Tia.

Soft weeping and sniffling sounded as he neared her room. He pressed open the door. "Tia?" His eyes took in her distress and then fell on the phone in her lap.

She tried to shove it under fairy-themed covers. Tears streamed down her face. She didn't bother swiping them away.

Ian rushed to her side. "Hey, sweetness, what's wrong?" Had she had a bad dream? Why did she have his phone? He'd left it in the hall to charge, on the wall table outside his bedroom.

Her lips trembled. "The phone made a funny sound. I got it because I thought it was Mommy." Huge eyes implored his. "I waited up for a long time, but she didn't call."

He leaned in and tried to give Tia a hug. She stiffened, so he backed away. "I'm sorry, Tia. I don't know what else to say."

Ian fought the urge to clench his fists and teeth over Ava having the gall to text and promise to call, then not. What was it with her? Couldn't she imagine what it was doing to her daughter?

Tia slid from the bed, grabbing a different set of clothes than the ones he'd picked out for her. Yet another sign she was pulling away. He fought despair. She clutched his phone to her chest. "May I see that for a second? I need to see who called."

She gave it to him, eyes shading as if scared he'd be angry. Ian pressed through the missed calls. Caleb. He read the corresponding text that explained there was no need to call him back, that he was just checking on things, namely his sister.

"Was it Mommy?" Tia looked half-hopeful.

Ian scooped her up. "I'm afraid not. Ready to

head to Miss Bri's? Daddy overslept this morning. I need to be at work soon."

"You said you were gonna have a day off." She scowled, poking him in the chest with every word.

"Maybe we'll go out for dinner tonight."

"I like that steak place."

Ian grinned. "You and Miss Bri."

"Can she go, too?"

Ian helped her on with her shoes. "Sure." Although with yesterday's weirdness, better to have a buffer. Maybe he'd invite some of the trauma center staff along, make it a group outing. He didn't often get to buy their dinners and wanted to.

They made their way to Bri's. Once there, he pulled Bri aside. "She's having a tough day. I know you can handle it, but if she gets too unruly or upset, call me?"

She nodded. "Don't worry. I'll have her cheered right up."

Ian looked Bri in her pretty eyes and knew without a doubt that was true. Five minutes in her presence and already he felt as though the weight of the world had lifted off his shoulders. "Thanks, Bri."

"For what?" Puzzlement flickered across her eyes as she hung Tia's jacket on her handcrafted hall tree. More and more of Tia's stuff was accumulating here. And more of their lives were becoming entwined over Tia's care.

"For just…being you. For being here. For both of us."

She nodded slowly, then raked fingers through her hair. He noticed faint lines around her eyes, as though she'd had a tough night's sleep, too. He probably shouldn't wonder why, but that didn't stop him from doing so.

He eyed the duck-themed calendar on Bri's wall. "Is the goose still stalking you on your runs?"

"Every time." Bri laughed. "I'm scared it will attack me."

"If I had someone to watch Tia, we could run together."

She met his gaze. "Thanks, but I'm perfectly capable of fending off an irate goose."

He grinned. "Well, I'm not so confident and the thing went after me the last morning I ran. Nearly got me, too." A flicker of vulnerability entered his gorgeous eyes. "Besides, I meant for the companionship more than for bodyguard services."

She blinked rapidly, not seeming to know how to respond. What was he doing, anyway?

"So, it's hard to believe tomorrow's New Year's Eve."

"I know. I hope the New Year is better than the last."

"I think it will be. Things are already looking up." When she turned to him, one look at her kind face and he knew she was one of the main reasons for that. "So, you're going to the New Year's Eve bash, right?"

"Of course. I wouldn't miss it for the world."

"Do you need a ride?"

"Oh, I hadn't thought about it. Yes, I probably will."

He fiddled with his watch, trying to stall. He could honestly say he'd rather skip work today and stand here talking to her all day. He scratched his jaw, suddenly feeling nervous about what he wanted to ask her. "So, you're gonna save a dance for me, right?"

Her eyes widened and her cheeks flushed an endearing pink. "Oh, well, sure. As long as you can guarantee it won't be the hokeypokey or the chicken dance."

He smiled at Bri, then Tia, off chasing Mistletoe. "She hits you up to dance to those, too, huh?"

"All day long. I think I hear those songs in my sleep."

He chuckled. Felt a sense of giddiness over the possibility of a slow dance tomorrow night. What a sweet way that would be to ring in the New Year and celebrate their friendship.

Or whatever this was between them. For once, Ian didn't feel dread or panic at the thought of it. Rather, hope.

A tentative, yet definite sense of joyful anticipation.

Bri cast him a shy smile below her long lashes. He felt no need whatsoever to try to hinder or hide his grin.

Mistletoe dragged Tia's sock off and ran under the table. Bri went to rescue it but couldn't maneuver well due to her cast.

"I got this." Ian knelt on the other side. Bri's floors smelled of wood polish and pine. He liked how clean she kept her house, yet it also seemed cozy, inviting and warm.

On his stomach now, Ian reached under her wagon-wheel coffee table and gently tugged the material from the puppy's sharp teeth. More because he knew it was good for the pup's teeth, and not because he was concerned about the dog shredding Tia's favorite socks. She had two more pairs just like them at home. Ian tugged the sock a little farther.

Mistletoe emitted a growl wannabe and lunged playfully, but his sharp teeth punctured Ian's thumb. Tia's dramatic falling over in a heap of giggles made the pain worth it, though. He doubted she realized the dog had just actually nipped him. "My daughter's favorite pair of fairy socks are not a chew toy, dog."

Tia giggled again as the tug-of-war continued over her sock.

His beeper went off. Then again. He stood, caught Bri's look as he eyed his pager. "That's Mitch. And Nita, our ward secretary, who's back for the winter while her husband is deployed."

"I love that you give precedence for employment to veterans and their families, Ian."

"That was Mitch's idea, actually." He scrolled through the message coming through. "Looks like we're already hopping this morning. I should go." He started to leave.

Tia leaped up from where she snuggled playfully with Mistletoe, who still gnawed on her sock. Tia scrambled to standing, one sock on and one off. "Wait! You forgot to ask her to dinner tonight."

Ian's ears warmed at the interest in Bri's eyes.

"Oh, yeah. Don't cook this evening because I'd like to take you and Tia to Golden Terrace."

She feigned a full-body melt. "Total yum! I'm game."

He smiled, waved at Tia and headed to the trauma center.

When he reached the door, Dr. Lockhart was getting out of her bright red sports car. He felt rude walking in, so he waited for her.

She seemed delighted to see him and jogged to catch up. She lifted her trendy purse over her shoulder, its sleek black color matching her hair. Funny, he'd always been attracted to dark-haired women before.

These days, though, it seemed blond was more his style.

"Good morning. What are your grand plans for the day?" she greeted him.

"Hopefully a slow day here, then a relaxing dinner with my daughter and our babysitter."

"Bri, right?"

Ian nodded, feeling almost dishonest by simply referring to her as his babysitter. She felt like more. "Bri's an amazing friend. I hope you get to know her." Now, even simply referring to Bri as "friend" felt off kilter.

The doctor smiled kindly. "I intend to. I could use some friends here in town. Kate and Lauren hit me up for my number yesterday and told me to expect to be called to join them for their upcoming girls-night-out to the drive-in. It's hard to believe there's still a town that has a drive-in."

"Yeah, Eagle Point is like that. So, have you ever been to Golden Terrace?" he found himself asking out of politeness.

"No, but I've heard they have to-die-for grilled shrimp."

"They do. All of their food is good. The fried

crawfish are a must." They entered the center and hung their lab coats up.

Her face pinched. "I think not."

He chuckled. "A few of us are getting together there after work hopefully. You're welcome to join us," Ian said, fully intending to invite the rest of the crew.

He didn't want Clara to feel left out, since she was new in town and in need of friends. Ian was glad Kate and Lauren planned to include her in their plans. He knew they were planning to ask Bri along, as well. Thankfulness filled him.

She hesitated a moment, then set her bag down on the nurses' station chair. Met his gaze. "Sure. If I wouldn't be intruding, I'd like that."

"No intrusion," he assured, waving at Kate, who came in still-damp hair through the employee entrance and headed to the time clock. Kate waved back and went about her day.

Dr. Lockhart smiled and pulled out her stethoscope to begin their patient rounds. Ian already felt the lightened workload and plummeted stress since her arrival. "Golden Terrace grilled shrimp in double portions, here I come."

Ian's grin was delicious, Bri thought to herself, about the one he'd cast ruefully over his wide shoulders upon departing ten minutes ago.

Bri turned back around and knelt to join Tia in

playing with the pup. She noticed Tia's eyes were red and puffy. "Do you have allergies, sweetie? Or is something wrong? You look like you've been crying."

"I'm crying because promises always break."

"Sometimes. It depends on the promise giver and the situation. Did someone break a promise to you?"

"They both did."

Bri assumed that "both" meant her parents. She needed to tread lightly here. Yet knew she needed to get to the root of Tia's anguish and reassure her. Maybe Tia misunderstood that Ian was still covering for Ava. In Bri's estimation, it was only serving to erode his relationship with Tia.

Lord, give me the words and Ian the wisdom to handle this.

That Bri suddenly felt like a partner in parenting Tia gave her a funny flip in her stomach. But, truthfully, it was a joint effort, since Tia's mom was willfully MIA and Bri was now Tia's primary female caregiver.

Bri set Mistletoe in his basket and reached for Tia. She scrambled willingly into Bri's lap. "Tia, I'm not sure what happened. I don't know your mom, but I do know your dad. He's the kind of person who always keeps his promises. If he doubts he can keep one, he won't make it in the first place. Trust me on that, okay?"

Skepticism fluttered across Tia's enormous eyes.

Bri brushed a comforting hand along Tia's back. "It's okay to hope for good things again. Okay?"

Tia's eyes watered. Her lips trembled. "Mommy didn't call." She uttered in such a fragile whisper, Bri barely heard it.

"Sweetie, what do you mean?" She strained to listen.

"She said she'd call and didn't again." Pain grew so pronounced in Tia's eyes; they resembled watery circles of sharded glass. *Again?* Bri had no idea what parental situation prompted Tia's raw words but Tia's composure fractured with them.

Bri pulled her swiftly in for a hug. "I'm so sorry. I can't promise you that your mom will call. But I can promise you that whether she does or not, life will look up. Good things and happy times will happen again soon."

Tia gathered a lock of Bri's hair and brushed her hand down it. "How do you know?"

"Because I believe in God and He says so. And He never, ever breaks a promise."

"How can He say so to me?"

"When you pray and listen. He speaks deep inside us. With words invisible to our ears that we hear with our hearts. He also promises through words in the Bible. Do you have one?"

"I don't know."

"Would you like one? I think it would cheer you up."

"What would cheer me up is if *you* were my mom instead of *her*."

Bri couldn't help the gasp. "Tia, don't say that."

"Well, it's true. I'm not dumb."

"You certainly are not." She pulled Tia's hair into a strand and began braiding, something her mom always did during heart-to-hearts. "Do you understand I'm only your babysitter?"

"I'm not a baby." Tia scrambled to cover Mistletoe with his blanket. She got his head, though, and he flailed and bucked his head until Bri discreetly tugged his face into view.

"Then I'm just your big-girl sitter. You know that, right?"

"I know that if you were my mom, you would have called."

If I were your mom, this wouldn't be a discussion because I wouldn't be stupid enough to break my daughter's heart or let a man like Ian go. Bri nearly gasped again. This time, at her own thoughts. She pulled Tia in for another hug.

"Tia, do you believe your dad will never leave

you? Because sometimes, it seems like you're scared he might."

"I don't care." She tossed Mistletoe's favorite tennis ball. He scrambled up and wobbled after it, nails clicking, then skidding on the tile. The ball was too big for his mouth, but he gave it a good try. Cute little growling sounds came out of him as he attempted to apprehend the fuzzy yellow ball.

"Yes, deep down you do. You might not want to care, but you do. Sometimes I pretend to be tough enough not to need anyone. Like my mom or dad or brother or friends. But truth is, I do. I think God gives us at least one solid person in our lives at all times, whom we and He knows will be there for us."

Oddly right now, that person was not Caleb, but Ian.

"I hope you will try to believe that solid person is your dad. He loves you very, very much."

Tia appeared to think about that. Bri hoped and prayed she'd take the words to heart.

"He likes chocolate," Tia said a while later as they folded a load of laundry together. "He needs it when he's grumpy."

"Is he grumpy to you?"

"No, he's grumpy to you. Maybe we should make him chocolate."

Bri burst out laughing. "Now, there's an idea."

They baked double-fudge cookies and Bri sprinkled a few extra chocolate chunks in the one Tia said was to be Ian's. After baking them, the pair bundled up themselves and Mistletoe in the new snowsuit Ian had purchased for him, and they set off to the trauma center.

Once inside, Kate pointed Bri to Ian's office. She knocked, suddenly feeling like an intruder. Dr. Lockhart sat across from him at his huge mahogany desk and they appeared to be going over a charting system.

"Hey, guys, come on in." Ian stood and smiled. Scooped Tia up, but again, she stiffened in his arms.

To her credit, she shoved the small cookie plate toward him. "That one's yours. No one else's. Got it?"

He bit his lip, Bri presumed to keep from grinning. "Got it."

Bri stepped across the floor, greeting Dr. Lockhart. "Nice to see you again." She really, really tried to mean it.

"You, as well." She barely acknowledged Bri though, and rather knelt, giving Tia her full attention. "Hello again."

"Hi," Tia said shyly. "You can have a cookie, too."

"Well, thank you very much. They look delicious. I'm sure your dad will like them, since he's so crazy about chocolate."

She knew that already? Bri fought insecurity. Over the doctor getting to know Ian and spending so much time with him. Also she seemed to be making an effort to reach out to Tia. Bri kicked herself mentally. The woman probably missed her daughter. Bri cast her a kind smile and this time truly meant it.

Once back at the cabin, Tia started helping Bri load her dishwasher. "Do you like my dad?"

Bri gulped. Helped Tia slide cups into the top rack. "He…well…we're friends. So of course I like him."

"I meant do you like him like a boyfriend. Because sometimes it seems like you do." Tia's eyes narrowed, resembling her dad's when he asked if her arm was hurting and she always denied it.

Bri gulped again. Odd how Tia had taken Bri's words and turned them around in a quest for information of Tia's own. "Well, I'm not sure yet," Bri answered honestly. "How would you feel if one day I told you I do?"

Tia's grin said more than her words ever could. But it made Bri feel anxious rather than elated. If Tia was getting her hopes up and something didn't happen, she was destined for heartache and so was Bri. Again.

She could handle her own heart breaking, but

to be responsible for heaping more pain on Tia's life? No way.

Lord, I need understanding as to what's going on here. Where Ian's concerned, I need Your wisdom on whether to hit the brakes or step on the gas. In Jesus's name, Amen.

Bri's new phone woke Tia from her nap. Especially since Bri couldn't remember how to answer it right away. Tia ran up and swiped the face, causing Bri to laugh. "Leave it to a kid to lead an adult through a technological crisis." Bri checked the missed-call menu, since it had already gone to voice mail. "That was your dad." Bri hoped he wasn't calling to cancel dinner. She hadn't set anything out to thaw. Soup would do, though, if so.

Bri hated her still-occasional pessimism. "Hello, sorry I missed your call."

"That's fine. I'm getting off in about ten minutes."

"We'll be ready."

"Awesome." A hesitation sounded in his voice, then, "We'll see you in a few."

We? Bri ended the call feeling numb dread travel up her arms. Especially given the weird vibe of Ian's hesitation.

Moments later, Ian knocked on her door. Bri opened it.

There stood Dr. Lockhart next to him. Bri

shuttered her shock, acutely aware of her simple slacks and nondescript shirt, compared to the stylish doctor's high-end name-brand clothing. "Please, come in."

Dr. Lockhart entered with Ian following more slowly. He paused in front of Bri and said in low tones, "Everyone else declined, saying they'd already made plans."

What did that mean? Bri eyed Ian quizzically but didn't ask. Did he sense her unease? He shouldn't worry about it. She was just being ridiculous. She shrugged it off and showed the lady doctor around her cabin.

"This is adorable," Dr. Lockhart was saying. "The wood is gorgeous, gleaming gold. I love your color selections."

"Thanks." Bri secured Mistletoe in his kennel. She thought she felt Ian's stare on her back, but didn't have any idea if Ian really studied her because she wasn't about to look at him.

They took the scenic route to the restaurant, Ian giving Dr. Lockhart the tour Bri had given him. Bri sat in the back with Tia and tried not to grit her teeth. They arrived at the restaurant in a half hour, after touring through Eagle Point.

Midway through dinner, Tia asked to get something out of the quarter machines in the front of the restaurant. Ian excused himself to take her. They stopped midway to speak to someone.

Instantly Dr. Lockhart's hand came across the table to cover Bri's. Bri froze, looked up. The woman's kind eyes canvassed Ian, whose back was to them, then she caught Bri's gaze. "I feel the need to reassure you that I'm not interested in Dr. Shupe. I respect him professionally, but that's the extent of my feelings and interest toward him."

Bri knew her mouth gaped. She tried to compose herself. "Oh. Well, it's none of my business, really. We're just friends."

The pretty doctor's mouth curved up in a rueful smile. "Mmm-hmm. That's exactly what he tried to tell me. Yet neither one of you can keep your eyes off the other when you think you're not looking."

Bri forgot to breathe. "No, I'm sure it's—"

"Oh, honey, I know the signs of deep and abiding care that precedes a complete romantic eclipse of the heart. I fell in love once. Stupidly, but still." Pain fluttered across her face, making it look strained, regretful and drawn.

"I'm certainly not in love with him," Bri blurted.

"Perhaps not yet. But I'd be remiss not to tell you that he talks about you *all* the time." The doctor sighed. Leaned in, imploring Bri to listen. "He's a good, good man, Bri. Take my advice, be patient. He's struggling now. But he'll come around. And when he does, I think you'll be pleasantly surprised at the man he is on the other side of his pain."

All Bri could do was be silent.

Dr. Lockhart watched Ian take Tia to the goodie machines. She faced Bri and continued, "He'll definitely be worth the wait. Plus, Tia adores you." Her eyes watered, causing Bri to turn her palm up and squeeze. Dr. Lockhart's hand trembled all the way to her fingers.

"Dr. Lockhart, I'm so sorry about your little girl," Bri whispered, voice going as raw as the agony in the doctor's eyes.

Smiling genuinely, she nodded. "Please, call me Clara. And when I'm able, I'll tell you about her sometime."

Bri squeezed her hand again. "I'd like that. I'd like us to be friends."

A humbly grateful expression lifted a layer of dismay from Clara's exceptionally pretty face. Her dark eyes brightened with wit. She released a tinkle of a laugh and patted Bri's hand. "Especially now that you know I'm not scoping out your man." She hiked a clandestine thumb Ian's way.

Bri's laughter died on her tongue. She blinked at Clara. Blinked at Ian.

Her man? Really?

As Bri's pulse skittered out of control when he

peered over his shoulder and disarmed her with one of his stellar smiles, she began to wonder if Dr. Lockhart's assessment was accurate, after all.

Chapter Fourteen

On the way to the car, Clara approached Ian. "Would you mind if Tia came to spend the night? I have some toys I'd like for her to go through. Even have a few fairy outfits she might like."

Ian realized the things had probably been her daughter's. And that she was having a tough time giving them up. "You won't have a hard time seeing them on another child?"

"No. It would bring me quite a bit of comfort. I can't see them going to waste, and I can't bear to take them to the consignment shop since no one else will get their sentimentality. You two get it, but not many others know." She indicated Bri, who stood on the sidelines out of the conversation.

Ian had seen the two women talking jovially, but he needed Bri to know he hadn't invited Clara because he was interested in her romantically.

Everyone else had already had dinner plans and he couldn't take back his invitation to the new doctor. Yet he was afraid Bri had been hurt by what he'd meant as an act of pure compassion, a friendly overture. He studied Clara. "I'm not sure she'll go with you."

Just then Tia skipped up. "Can I go to Miss Lockhart's house? She has fairy clothes and toys."

"Sure you won't get scared at night?"

"No. I'm a big girl," Tia said bravely. Ian decided to let her go with Clara, even though he had a feeling Tia would wake up scared.

He passed Clara his cell number. "Just call me if I need to come get her."

She nodded. "I will. Thanks, Ian."

He nodded and wished Bri's house wasn't first on the road. He dropped her off and walked her to her cabin. "Hey, you okay?"

"Of course. Why wouldn't I be?"

He studied her carefully. She seemed to be telling the truth. "Okay, then, I'll catch you later."

He drove Tia and Clara to Clara's lakeside house, two down from Ellie's. He walked them in, surprised when Tia didn't panic. She waved him away and skipped excitedly into Clara's home.

Ian pulled into his own driveway, but couldn't stand the thought of sitting in a dark house alone.

He really, really wanted to make sure Bri was okay. He peered through his trees, over the lake, past the trauma center. The faint glow of her cabin lights let him know she was still awake.

After driving over, he knocked lightly and said, "Bri, it's Ian."

She opened the door swiftly. "What's wrong?" She peered behind him as though looking for someone else. He noticed she was in her pajamas. Had he dragged her out of bed?

"Tia's at Clara's." He raked a hand across the back of his neck. "I'm not even sure why I'm here. Don't know why I got you up. This is— Look, I'm sorry. I should let you sleep."

She smiled and folded arms across her chest. "Ian Shupe, you are absolutely adorable in a confounded state."

He blinked. She tugged her robe tight and slipped into her foyer, waving toward her country cabin-style seating. "You've obviously got something on your mind, so come on in and sit a bit." She sat and motioned to the place across from her. Rather than sit, he took her hands and pulled her up and very close.

The surprising motion made her gasp. He held tightly to her hand and gaze. "This might not be the time or the place, and I don't mean to put you in a position of questioning my propriety, but I've just gotta get something off my chest."

"Okay. I'm listening."

"With your ears or your heart?"

She blinked. "Both, if you want me to."

He nodded, then leaned in without reservation and kissed her softly on the cheek. His lips trailed a breezy path from her cheekbone to her ear. He tightened his hold of her and grinned. "I don't kiss my friends on the cheek. Ever."

She squeezed his hands back. "Okay. So…"

"So, I don't know what else to say except I need you to hang in there with me."

She nodded. Then, to his surprise and delight, pulled her hands from his and wrapped her arms around his neck in a hug so strong no distance remained between them, emotionally or physically. "Ian, I'm not going anywhere. Unless it's with you."

"But I've been—"

"I don't care. None of that matters now." She leaned into his embrace, his vulnerability, his strength. "I'm right here."

He folded his hand in a clutch and pressed it to his chest. "You're right here, too. Deep in my heart."

If Mitch could hear this, he'd razz Ian big-time. Tell him to go audition for writing greeting cards or something. But Ian didn't care. She needed to know how he felt. Last thing he wanted to do was lose her over a misunderstanding.

He felt sudden moisture against his face. He leaned back. His chest felt cracked in two at her tears. "You're crying."

She shook her head and smiled so sweet and so brightly, he wouldn't have been surprised to see her silly bird-clock come to life behind her. "I'm happy. Overwhelmed with joy. Surprised. Scared, but willing. You don't know how much I care about you, Ian. And Tia? She's icing on the cake."

He smiled. "You seemed so unsure when you saw Clara at the door earlier. I needed to come reassure you."

She smiled. "Believe me, I'm reassured. I'm glad you're reaching out to her. We had a heart-to-heart. She knows, well, that we're slightly more than friends."

"I'm glad you could finally admit that." He grinned. Wanted to kiss her for real. But it was late, the hallway dark. "So, forward?"

Without hesitation, she hugged him. "Forward."

He gave himself over to the hug, surprised at the feelings that crackled between them. Took everything in him not to follow through on that kiss.

He almost succeeded in resisting, too. Until she tilted her beautiful face up with the lush smile and killer eyes that got him every time. Why bother fighting it?

Just as Ian dipped his head to kiss Bri, his pager went off. He seriously thought about tossing it in the lake.

He sighed, taking in Bri's ruddy cheeks and winsome eyes. He read the message of an incoming air trauma. "I can honestly say this is one time I wish I weren't a doctor. Too many interruptions of important things." He brushed a tender gaze along her face, down her chin and back up. "But I'm hoping you'll give me a rain check of this very moment?"

Her eyes looked both apprehensive and hopeful. "Maybe at the New Year's dance?"

Her words held question and answer, promise and faith, and he found himself peering past her long lashes and drawn to drown in the bliss of blue. Stunning shape and color, yes, but even more magnetic was the sensation that literal hope glittered at him through her lovely eyes.

He'd almost kissed her! Bri fairly floated to the doorway of her bedroom. She tucked Mistletoe's blanket up under his chin and he fell instantly back to sleep. "You sleep as much as a newborn."

Her phone rang. She smiled to see Ian's gorgeous grin gracing her smart screen. "Hello?"

"Hey." Bri could hear the smile in his voice. "I'm kind of in a bind. Clara has to answer the pages now, too."

Bri leaped up. "Oh! I'll run and get Tia."

"Thanks, Bri. I knew I can count on you. If you would just take Tia to my house so she can sleep in her own bed? I have a feeling it's going to be a long night."

"I don't know how you function, Ian."

"It's called power naps. I slept for several hours today."

"Okay. That makes me feel better." Bri slipped her shoes on and dashed across the trauma center lot, Ian still on the phone.

"I want to make sure those coyotes don't get ya."

She smiled. "I have a high-caliber flashlight. But I do admit I'll be glad when I am able to drive again."

"A few weeks. In the meantime, feel free to crash at my place whenever I have to call you over to watch Tia in the middle of the night. Clean linens and extra blankets are in the second hall closet."

"I can manage. I see the helicopter approaching the trauma center, so I'll let you go." She hung up, realizing he hadn't wanted to get off the phone any more than she did.

Bri met Clara in the brick-lined asphalt driveway. Tia was asleep in her arms. "Thank you, Bri. I didn't even think about this."

"Not a problem. I'm happy to help."

"On the upside, Tia has some nice new outfits and a few more noisy toys to drive her dad crazy with." Clara carried Tia into Ian's living room and set her on the couch.

Bri smiled. "I guarantee he'll send all the noisy toys to my house."

Clara grinned and threw her stethoscope around her neck. "Well, when you move in here after you and Ian get married, you'll have your just revenge."

Bri felt her eyes bug. She shook her head. "I can see that Kate has gotten to you."

Clara peered out Ian's back French doors. "There's the chopper. I better get over there."

After Clara left, Bri went to move Tia to her room. She realized she couldn't lift her safely with her arm, hence the reason Clara had carried Tia in.

Bri pulled blankets and pillows out and made herself a pallet on the opposite end of the couch. Tia blinked groggy eyes at her, then snuggled up close, tucking her hair under Bri's chin.

As Tia's tiny arms wound around Bri's neck, maternal instincts roared to life in Bri. She kissed Tia on the forehead and smoothed hair out of her eyes. "I love you, sweetness," she whispered.

Tia's arms tightened around her neck. "I'm praying hard for you to be my new mom."

Bri closed her eyes and hugged Tia tight,

knowing she was praying the same exact prayer. Bri attempted to stay awake, but sleep beckoned and she drifted off, still snuggled with a little fairy girl.

Ian had never seen a more beautiful, touching sight. Bri slept with Tia next to her heart. Tia's head rested on Bri's shoulder and Bri's chin against Tia's head. They both slept deeply, Bri with a bit of a snore.

He smiled. Took out his phone and snapped a photo. He'd make Bri a memory book for Valentine's Day.

He marveled at the closeness his daughter and Bri shared. Tia responded to Bri like no one else. Not even Kate had managed that kind of rapport in so little time.

Ian reached a hand out and tugged a church bulletin from the Bible Bri must've brought over and left open. He noted the service times and his promise to Tia to help her make friends.

Ian knew the Lord was the best friend to have. In that moment, he determined in his heart to bring her to church, starting this Sunday. To make sure she grew up knowing God and having faith that would sustain no matter what. Ian settled back into his recliner, knowing there were only a couple more hours until sunrise. No sense in waking Bri now. He'd let her sleep.

In fact, he felt drowsy, too. He leaned back and closed his eyes. A sound opened his eyes.

Tia was awake and standing at the foot of his recliner. "Bri snores. I can't sleep around it." She scowled groggily.

Ian chuckled. "Would you like to climb up here with me?"

She blinked tentatively at the couch and Bri. Ruddy noises vibrated from her throat now. Tia looked back at Ian and nodded. "Yes. I'm a sleepy bug."

"That's okay. It's still early." It was the greatest feeling in the world when Tia reached out her hands to be lifted up. He pulled her close and she didn't stiffen. Better still, she rested her head on his shoulder. Within a few minutes, little snoring sounds breezed out of her, too.

Ian smiled. Tia and Bri were so much alike he could see how people would mistake them for mother and daughter. Bri would make a wonderful, caring mom. *And an amazing wife.*

Ian closed his mind from the thought, but didn't dare give in to sleep. He held Tia tighter and relished the closeness while he could. It seemed she was warming up to him and trusting more. Hopefully this wasn't just nighttime stupor and desperation for sleep that caused Tia to come close to him.

He put his hand on her back and wished again like crazy he was a praying-out-loud kind of man.

If you were, what would you say?

The thought popped into his head. He cleared his throat and needed to get the words out.

"I'd say thank you for giving her to me. I'd say watch over her and keep her safe. Let her know how much I love her." He brushed Tia's hair aside and breezed a kiss on her forehead.

"Wuv you, too, Daddy," Tia murmured in a groggy voice, and hugged him tighter around the neck.

The worst day in the world could not strip Ian's smile or stop joy from detonating inside. Three sweet words. "Thank you," Ian said to them both.

A sense of peace descended like the snow had last week over Eagle Point and all its farmland. God had taken his words like an offering and counted them as a prayer.

Ian swallowed when Tia snuggled even closer. He wanted to pray aloud again, but didn't want to wake her. In his head, he said, *Thank You. Forgive me for my anger these past months. I was wrong about You. I want to know and love You rightly. To have a thankful heart instead of a hateful one.*

After praying, Ian wondered if he should have gone ahead and said it out loud. Tia needed to see him living for God.

He'd picked up a Bible for himself when he'd gotten Tia one. Ian realized he'd been approaching God with the same mistrust Tia had for him. He'd been flailing against God, only no purple tutu. Just flat-line faith and doubt and disillusionment. He'd been swirling in it so long, he felt as if his life had turned into a toilet.

I want to be the kind of man she can look up to. A man worthy of the honor and respect I see in Bri's eyes, even when I'm grouchy. I really don't understand why I do that. But I know I want to change. "And one last thing. When Tia's sixteen, help me not punch out the first guy who shows up at the door. Amen."

Of all the things Ian was looking forward to, his daughter's first date definitely wasn't it.

There was one date he was looking forward to, however.

The New Year's Eve bash in downtown Eagle Point, where he had the pleasure of accompanying the most beautiful woman in town.

Chapter Fifteen

Wow. Total stunner.

Ian took in Bri's sparkly silver-and-sapphire sequined dress when she answered the door the next evening.

Kate had caught wind of Ian picking Bri up and had picked Tia up early from Bri's, saying she wanted to take her shopping for a special New Year's Eve dress.

Ian had the feeling Kate was arranging a matchmaking plan, however. This time, he couldn't say he minded.

"Wow. Don't you look handsome." Bri ran a hand along Ian's tuxedo lapel and met his eyes with a smile. "Very nice."

He smiled and ran his gaze from her classy coifed hair to her high-heeled shoes. No clue how she planned to dance in them, but the way they complimented her already attractive legs made him not care one iota. "Shall we?" He took her hand and led her down the steps.

"Your hair is gorgeous like that, Bri."

Her cheeks tinged. "Thank you. Clara came over and fixed it for me."

"I knew she'd left a little early."

"I hope you all don't get called in to work tonight."

"We brought some rent-a-docs and nurses in. No one in Refuge or Eagle Point wants to miss this night."

"I so wish Mama could see it. To know how two communities plus a military base and a Guard unit came together this week to save the lodge." Bri's eyes turned glassy and he knew she fought bittersweet joy and tears. He squeezed her hand, just now realizing he still held it on the way to his car.

He helped her inside, tucking her black, fringy shawl over her shoulder so it wouldn't get caught in the door. His fingers brushed her shoulder and their eyes met.

He wasn't in any hurry to move his gaze or his fingers. "You look lovely. Absolutely stunning."

Now her face flamed red. "Thank you. You're quite the looker yourself, all gussied up in that tux."

He grinned the entire walk to his truck's driver's side and drove as slow as possible to the dance. Once they got among the crowd, everyone would swarm her since her lodge was essentially the reason for the party. So for the few moments' drive into town, he wanted her all to himself.

The crowd converged on their car as if they were Hollywood A-list actors and the crowd were paparazzi, minus the cameras. Instead of being inundated with flash photography, she was engulfed in hugs instead.

Ian chuckled at the exuberance of the town. Since Kate and Tia weren't scheduled to be here for another twenty minutes, Ian wove through the mingling crowd and took in all the merriment and sparkly decor.

The band was gearing up to play, but for now lively carnival-style music blared from overhead speakers. Lights were strung from one end of the square to the other, and met in the middle over a huge welded truss that made the square seem covered in light. Faux ivory with white lights twined through it covered the brick columns in the square's enormous octagon patio.

As Ian approached what had to be a special children's section, kid-friendly music thumped from speakers there. A smaller stage and a table with judging chairs sat in preparation for a kids' dance contest.

Meanwhile, several huge cardboard silver-and-gold stars leaned against the walls, where kids would run to them and spin them round and round. Then the announcer would choose a number and the child with that numbered star would win a prize. Ian smiled that there were enough stars to last the evening and enough prizes that all children would get at least one. Bri would love this. Ian peered around, but she had disappeared in the festivities.

His phone vibrated. "Hello?"

"Guess what?"

Ian was surprised to hear Tia's voice excitedly on the line. "What?"

"I got fairy wings with my new dress! It's rainbow and sparkly!"

"How exciting! I'm sure you look lovely in it. I can't wait to see it. Are you having fun with Kate?"

"Yes, but I miss Bri and wish she was here."

He knew the feeling. He looked around, but she was nowhere in sight. "I gotta go," Tia was saying. "We gotta get shoes."

"You have a new pair of sandals."

"Not for me, silly. Kate needs shoes."

Ian knew about Kate's shoe addiction and laughed. "Somehow I highly doubt that. But have fun shopping, anyway."

"We will. She says to hush and we'll see you in ten."

Ian chuckled. "See you in ten." Ian hung up

and went to the food tables. Colorful appetizers and finger foods were displayed banquet-style on catering tables. "I heard they donated this food for free," a pleasant voice said behind him.

He turned, an instant smile on his face. Bri. She plucked an olive and a piece of cheese off his plate. "You weren't planning to eat without me, were you?"

He grinned. "I don't know. I wasn't sure I'd see you again this evening."

Mischief sparked in her eyes. "Are you kidding? I've been asked to dance by the cutest guy here. No way am I missing out on that."

He felt his ears grow warm. He looked around and feigned ignorance. "Who's the lucky guy?"

"You, silly." She sidled up next to him and peered at his plate. "Whatcha got there?"

"Caleb warned me about you." He nodded to the clean plates. "How about you get your own?"

She plucked an oval cracker and dipped it in a spoonful of soft cheese he'd put on his plate. "It's more fun to share."

He swerved his plate away playfully. "You mean steal?"

She giggled and went for her own plate, but his hand stopped hers. "Actually, I'd rather share." He let her put items on his plate, then led her to one of several dozen white wrought-iron tables at the west end of the square. "Sweet tea?" he asked, the drink she liked.

"You know it." She tugged her shawl over her cast and smiled. He knew she had a follow-up appointment coming and hoped things were healing well. Seemed to be.

Ian brought back their drinks and sat across from her, just then realizing how small the tables were. His knees brushed hers. "Sorry." He gave her a wry grin but didn't try to find a better way to sit. He loosened his tie and considered moving his knees, since the silky feel of her leg was wreaking utter havoc with his senses. "Where's Tia?"

"She's with Kate. They're shopping."

Bri rolled her eyes. "Oh, brother. I've been shopping with the two of them. One day when Kate and Lauren came to pick me up, the last time we had a girls' night out. Kate and Tia are total shoe-aholics, and if they end up anywhere near a shoe store, they're liable not to get here until the New Year's bash is nearly over."

"You're probably right." Ian's ears perked up as a slow song came on. He peered at Bri. She stared at his plate, cheeks tinged. He reached for her hand. "May I?"

She shook her head. "Not yet. I've been so nervous about this evening, I haven't eaten all day.

My blood sugar is so low right now, I'd likely pass out in the middle of our dance."

He nodded and went to refill a second plate. She laughed when he put it in front of her. Kate texted him to say she and Tia were having so much fun shopping, they might be later than expected. Ian figured Kate was just keeping Tia away because she wanted him and Bri to have some time alone.

That suited him just fine. Not that he didn't want to see his daughter. He was having fun spending time with Bri.

Two minutes before midnight, another slow song came on. "Come on. This will probably be the last one."

She settled her hand in his and he led her to the dance floor, totally not caring who saw. She felt good and right in his arms as the music began. They danced respectably and Ian smiled when she rested her cheek on his shoulder. "I like it when you lean on me."

"I'm thankful God sent you to lean on."

"I'm beginning to believe it."

She smiled. "I knew. Tia told me you bought her a Bible and promised to take her to church."

He nodded, then leaned his head back to peer when Bri drew a shaky breath. "You okay?"

Her eyes flitted away for a moment, then back

to his. "Yeah. I made a phone call while Tia was napping today."

"Yeah? What's that?" Ian dipped her, causing hair to spill over his arm.

He lifted her back up and wished like crazy to pull her closer. But they were still hovering somewhere between friendship and more. And right now, he couldn't completely define the more.

"Yeah, I called the nursing home. Spoke to my dad."

He paused, even though the music continued. "How'd it go?" He resumed their gentle sway.

She drew a breath. "I'm not sure he remembered me." Pain made her eyes a stormy shade of blue. Yet he saw a peace residing there that hadn't been before. "But I promised to come see him, anyway. He has memory loss from a brain injury, but I have to try."

"I'm really proud of you, Bri. I'm happy to go with you, if you want me to."

"I'd like that. Thank you, Ian." Disappointment hit him that the song was winding down. Ian swept her beneath a shade tree and held her close. Too soon, she whispered something about needing to find the ladies' room, so Ian reluctantly let her go.

Once it was about time for Kate and Tia to show, he searched around for them. He wanted to see the fancy dress Tia had called excitedly to tell him about.

Her call had surprised and delighted him. Tia had chattered on and on, seeming to forget for those few moments that she was supposed to be mad at him. He knew he needed to tell her the truth about her mom soon.

Just not tonight. Tonight he'd let her enjoy herself and feel like the princess she believed she was.

Ian looked around for Tia but decided Kate must not have arrived with her yet. Mitch approached with a grin. "Wow. Everyone looks way different out of scrubs and camouflage."

Ian nodded and went to the punch table, hoping for a sighting of Tia or Bri. He didn't feel whole without either of them. The truth hit him like a war missile. He met Mitch's eyes. "Dude, I'm falling hard."

Mitch looked at him funny. "Not sure what that means, Shupe. No one spiked the punch."

Ian shook his head. "No, I mean Bri."

Mitch's eyes widened, but not as much as Ian would have expected. "No surprise there." He chinked his cup against Ian's. "Congrats, man. I'm happy for you."

"I don't know. Maybe I need to step back a little."

Mitch grew serious. "If you're asking my opinion, I say no. I think you should step forward. She's a great girl."

"I think so, too. Seen her lately?"

"No, actually. Not since we first arrived. Maybe she's with Lauren." But when Lauren approached with Bri not at her side, Ian started to worry.

"Let. Me. Go." Bri seethed words through her teeth and Eric's skin-crushing grip.

He leaned in, the smell of whiskey strong on his breath. "This is an open party. You can't stop me from being here." He stumbled precariously. Bri tried again to jerk her arm free. She nearly lost her balance.

His face hardened to the point of scaring her. "I've been keeping up with your little lodge-saving party through the Four Dogs blog."

Bri fought annoyance. And fear. She looked around for Ian. Mitch. Kate. Anyone who'd see she might be in trouble. She'd gone to the re-stroom to check her makeup, and he'd lunged out of the shadows between two of Eagle Point's buildings. *"Four Guys, a Dog and a Blog,"* Bri corrected.

His gaze narrowed. "I don't appreciate being corrected." He increased the pressure of his hand, causing her to cry out. "And I don't appreciate being dumped by a half-wit who didn't appreciate how good she had it."

"Let her go."

Bri whirled. Eric's head whipped around.

Ian moved like a freight train to put himself between her and Eric. He didn't bother asking Bri if this guy was giving her trouble. Rather, Ian gripped Eric's arm much the same way he did Bri. Ian squeezed until Eric's face contorted in pain. He let go of Bri's arm as though it were a venomous snake. Eric tried to stumble backward, but Ian held fast, still gripping his arm. Hard. Harder.

"You like that? How's it feel to be bullied by someone bigger than you?" Ian towered over Eric, and Bri could see the combat-trained military man he must have learned to hide well in a civilian setting.

Eric crumbled to his knees, gave Bri a helpless look, then anger flashed in his eyes. "Call your boyfriend off."

"He's not my—" Bri's mouth clamped shut at the question in Ian's eyes. She faced Eric. "It's none of your concern who he is to me. You need to leave now or I'll have you arrested." She rubbed her arm, causing Ian's gaze to fall there.

Ian picked up his phone, and Bri knew without a doubt he was calling the sheriff. The rage forming in Ian's eyes as he watched the bruise erupt on Bri's arm made her realize the level of self-control Ian must have used not to punch Eric in the nose.

Because Ian sure looked like he wanted to.

"Yeah, Sheriff? Bri Landis has been assaulted in an alley between Sully's and Golden Terrace. She's okay, but her arm is bruised pretty good. No, I got the guy. Her ex-boyfriend decided to crash the party."

Eric tried to twist out of Ian's grasp. He spat at the ground when he couldn't. Bri almost laughed that Ian didn't even appear to be straining or winded. His strength surpassed what she could have imagined. And Eric was no wimp. She rubbed her arm as a testament.

"She won't press charges," Eric bit out and smirked at Bri. "She never did."

"You never hurt me like this before. Only with words."

Eric's answer was a sneer. "You don't have the guts to have me arrested. Call your dog of a boyfriend off. Or I'll have my attorney arrest both of you."

Ian snorted laughter. "You must be tanked. Tell me, did you drive here? Because if you did, I have a feeling the sheriff is going to find open alcohol in your car."

The sheriff and several Refuge and Eagle Point officers ran over on foot with handcuffs drawn.

Bri looked Eric squarely in the eyes and said, "He bruised my arm and shoved me against the building. He pulled my hair, then wouldn't let me leave willingly. I'd like to have him arrested for assault and battery."

Eric squealed like a girl as the cops hauled him to his feet. He tried to get away from the police, who then ended up dragging him across the alley toward their blinking car.

Now, suddenly alone in Ian's presence, Bri felt complete and utter shame. He'd seen her weak. She put her head down. "I need a moment alone."

His hand came up to cup her face. "He hurt you."

"I'll be fine."

He swallowed. "Bri, please don't shut me out."

She shook her head. "I said, I want to be alone."

Ian's hands trembled as it gently encircled her wrist, then her arm. "I'm sorry I wasn't here sooner to protect you. You need to follow through with pressing charg—"

"I intend to," she snapped. But she was on the verge of tears and shame that she'd never known before.

Why had Eric come back? Doubtful he'd have nerve to return again. That wasn't what scared her.

What scared her was that she'd stupidly opened her heart to another man. Especially one prone to beastly moods.

She eyed Ian. Knew that wasn't completely fair.

But right now, it was the only thing that felt safe.

"Goodbye, Ian." She turned and ran to find someone to drive her home. She could not face Ian. Moreover, she could not face her feelings for him.

She'd made a tremendous mistake.

One that could hurt Tia.

No way could Bri forgive herself for that. She obviously wasn't ready to take things to another level. Hot tears streamed down Bri's cheeks as she tried to figure out how to get home.

She saw Brock up ahead, getting into his car. She ran up, swiped her raccoon eyes away.

He leaned out, looking on high alert at her rapid approach. "Brock, I need a favor. I'm not feeling well. Can you give me a ride home?"

"Hop in." He noticed her hair was a mess from her encounter with Eric. "What happened to you? Where's Ian?"

She shook her head, feeling on the verge of a breakdown over the mention of Ian's name. Of the hurt displayed in his eyes with her words. "Please, don't ask questions. Just drive."

"Just drive," Ian told Mitch. Lauren had found out about the incident and had told Kate that Ian went to look for Bri.

"Someone said she left with Brock."

"She needs to go to the cop shop and put the jerk away."

"I agree. But I've never seen her so vulnerable and broken. It was like all the verbal abuse came back full force, washing away her common sense. Her ability to think clearly."

"Be patient, Ian. Like you, she'll come around."

"I don't intend to give up or stop reaching out to her until she does."

Bri's lights were off in her cabin by the time they made it there. Ian passed Brock's truck in the driveway. He nodded a greeting and gave Ian a thumbs-up as they passed on the road.

"Wait here. Let me talk sense into her."

Bri curled up on the couch and wiped her streaked makeup off with a cloth. A light tapping at her door nearly caused her to shriek.

Eric had scared her. More than anyone would ever know.

She'd had Brock run her by the police station and she'd filled out a formal report. The officers assured her Eric would not be bothering her tonight or any other night, and they'd keep her place heavily patrolled.

Plus Bri had no doubt once Caleb heard, he'd have the Guard monitoring every inch of her property. She smiled ruefully and tried to ignore whoever was at the door.

They were persistent enough she dragged herself off the couch and poked her head between the crack.

Ian. While one part of her wanted to slam the door on him and everything he'd come to mean to her, another part of her wanted to unlatch the chain lock and fall into the strength and safety of his arms.

"Are you gonna let me in?"

"Are you gonna leave the second I ask you to?"

His jaw tensed. "If that's the only way you'll let me in."

She flipped the chain and swung open the door. He stepped in gingerly, his cologne reminding her of how he'd held her in the dance. Carefully. Respectfully. Same way his eyes held her now.

Nothing like Eric.

"May I sit?"

She indicated the couch. "Suit yourself."

Rather than react to her with harsh words, he looked as if he could scoop her close and kiss the world out from under her feet.

Her brain fogged up as his hands came up to cup her shoulders. Bri swayed into him as he bent to brush a kiss as soft as velvet across her lips. Then stopped short as sense returned. Their eyes widened in an unexpected, electric moment. They both skittered backward like startled forest squirrels. "I should—"

"Go get Tia—"

Ian turned and took off so fast she'd have thought the trauma sirens were going off. The ones inside her head were.

It took a few deep breaths for Bri to fully recover and figure out exactly what had just happened.

Because truth was, she really liked kissing Ian.

Why did she feel so powerfully drawn to him? This attraction seemed a force all its own.

Perhaps their mutual concern for Tia and her emotional plight created a powerfully swift and unexpected bond. But what if it was more? Was God up to it? Was it stupid to hope so?

"Lord, times like this make me really miss Mama. I know You will sustain me. Like You, Lord, she was the best listener in the world." Bri paced, fighting sadness inside her chest. Then Bri stopped, realizing she'd picked up that quirk from Ian.

Her heart softened at the thought of his name. How deeply she'd come to care for him hit her with the force of a tsunami wave. There was a knock on her door. Two guesses who it was.

"Ian, I'm really tired. Can we please talk about this tomorrow?"

Clearly he wasn't keen on leaving her alone. "I started to leave but couldn't. I just want to be sure you're okay. That you don't need to be seen by a doctor."

"*You're* a doctor. It's just a tiny bruise."

"No, it's five bruises from his hand nearly crushing your arm."

"It won't happen again."

"How can I be sure?"

She opened her front door. "Because I'm never letting him, or any man, get close enough to hurt me again. Now, if you'll excuse me, I just want to sleep."

He stared at her for several moments with such determination and intensity, Bri was surprised when surrender weighed his shoulders down.

Wordless, he sauntered out, turning back to cast a tender but still determined look. "I'll see you tomorrow."

"Will Tia be over?"

He paused on the landing, fingers shoved into his pockets. "No. She's staying the night with Kate."

Bri nodded. "I'll still be able to watch her, though, right?"

Ian's jaw tensed. "Possibly for now, but she's getting too attached to you."

Tears flooded Bri's eyes, because she knew.

She knew with her whole mind, soul and heart that he was right.

"Good night, Ian." Bri closed the door feeling as if she'd just set into motion two more wretchedly painful goodbyes.

Chapter Sixteen

"Daddy, I miss her." Tia said to Ian on the drive back from his mom's three weeks into the New Year.

"I miss her, too." In fact, Ian had not been able to stop thinking of Bri for two solid weeks. Before that, he'd endured a week of utter misery when Bri all but avoided him the first week of the New Year, except for impersonal nods and a monotone report of Tia's behavior for the day.

Ian hated the shadows Eric's attack had etched into Bri's eyes when he'd dropped off or picked up Tia. Finally, after a solid week of anguish and uncertainty, he'd turned the reins over to Dr. Lockhart and taken a much-needed two weeks off.

"Did you have fun on the Disney cruise?" Ian pulled onto the road leading to his home.

"Yeah. I'm glad Grandma and Grandpa went

with us. And my aunts and uncles. But, I wish Miss Bri coulda gone."

Ian hadn't bothered asking her, because he knew she'd say no. She'd thwarted every effort to build on what they'd started.

On the upside, Kate had texted him that Bri had started going to counseling two days after he'd gone on vacation. Ian dragged his suitcase out of the back of his truck, then Tia's.

"Can we go get Mistletoe and see Miss Bri now?"

"He's right here."

Ian looked up. Bri sat on his doorstep, waiting with the dog. He froze, not knowing what to make of it. Was she resigning as his sitter? Handing over the dog? Disappearing from their lives for good?

Bri held her arms out to Tia, who rushed her on first sight. "Briiii!"

Ian couldn't help but smile, yet it felt bittersweet.

He approached cautiously and realized under his porch light that Bri's eyes were red and blotchy.

He leaned in. "Are you having an allergic reaction?"

Her chin wobbled and she shook her head. Handed the squirmy dog to Tia and stepped close.

"No. I—I just missed you and Tia. So, I decided to come sit on your porch."

Ian didn't hide his grin. "Like, today?"

A shy look came across her face. "No, every day since you left, actually. Let's walk."

Ian took Tia's hand as they started down the street. "I've been going to see a counselor about stuff with Eric."

"So I heard."

"Well, I realize now how irrational I've been. How silly it was to compare the two of you. I also have been seeing you and Tia leaving the early church service when I'm driving in for the later one. I'd like us to…to go together from now on." A vulnerability shone in her true-blue eyes.

Ian paused to pick up the dog, who was having a tough time keeping up with long people-legs. Tia ran to his side yard to fetch the ball for the dog.

Ian took the opportunity to touch Bri's arms. "I'm not that guy, Bri. The brooding man who's insensitive and crude."

"I know. I realize that now. I guess I was just afraid."

"And now?"

"I'm not scared of you, only scared of losing you. And Tia."

Ian felt like shouting joy. Tia rushed up and

dragged their hands. "Come on! Let's play fairy checkers."

On the way in, Bri faltered at the door. Ian wrapped a reassuring arm around Bri. "You look worried," he explained. "I might have been a fool in the beginning, but I'm fully in my senses now. Okay?"

"I'm glad to hear you say that."

"But?" he asked.

"True fairy tales are hard to find."

Ian shook his head. "I used to think so, too."

"But now?"

"I think I'm looking Happily Ever After right in her gorgeous blue eyes."

"Ready for today?" Kate asked Bri, two days after she'd had her cast removed.

"Boy, am I. My first Eagle Point 5K run since I left for college in Chicago, and I have a scar the size of a shoestring."

"You can't see it. I'm just glad you feel like running. Who's watching Tia again?"

"Clara and Ian's mom. She drove down to see him cross the finish line. She says she wants to see which one of us beats the other across that line." Bri giggled but noticed Kate was some-what subdued.

"You need to go slow. Not try to win. Just try to finish."

"I know. But it would still be nice to win against Ian." Yet even saying it, Bri knew it wasn't true.

Where there'd always been an air of competition between herself and Eric, Bri truly wanted Ian to prosper. "I hope he wins."

"Oh, believe me. He will."

Kate finished adjusting her shoes and they took their places at the front. Bri felt relieved that Ian's mom and Clara had taken Tia to the library today to do some reading. Communication ceased as they ran Lem's fundraiser race.

As Bri approached the finish line, it didn't say Finish Line, or even The End. It said, Bri Landis, Will You Marry Me?

Tears rushed her eyes. Ian stood at the finish line with a pensive expression, and she realized that every runner had pulled off the road except for her and Kate.

Her hands went to her cheeks when she realized they'd rigged the whole race to prepare for Ian's proposal.

"Oh. My." Tia giggled beside Ian's mom, as Ian flipped the ribbon up and stepped under it, approaching Bri like a man on a serious mission. Two steps away from her, he looked very nervous as he knelt on one knee.

Bri gasped at the same time. The crowd must

have taken that as a positive sign, with cheers and clapping ensuing.

Ian stood and held up his hands. "Hold up, people! I haven't asked her yet." Ian led Bri across the track, to a private spot under Tia's favorite jungle gym. The world dwindled to just the two of them as he captured her lips in a kiss that made her heart soar.

Bri swayed when the kiss ended. And clung to the material of Ian's track shirt. He grinned down at her, but by no means looked down on her. Never again would she mistake Ian's subdued mannerisms for Eric's deplorable ones.

Ian nodded behind Bri. She turned to find Tia rushing up with Mistletoe. Tia set Mistletoe in Bri's arms, then dashed past her to her dad and hugged him around the legs. He hugged her back but kept his eyes on Bri. "Turn his tag around."

Bri gasped and squealed louder than Tia. The puppy's tail wagged. Tears filled Bri's eyes as Tia scrambled close. "What is it?"

"I—I think it's a ring." She peeled the packaging off as Ian came close and pulled her in.

"Bri, you know I don't make promises and certainly don't make promises I can't keep. But as sure as I'm here today, I promise you that as long as there is breath in me, I will love you."

"I will love you, too, Ian."

Then he knelt to one knee again. "So, you'll

make me the happiest, luckiest guy on earth and marry me?"

She threw herself around his neck. "Yes! Oh, yes."

Tia giggled behind them and knelt in front of the puppy. "Me and Mistletoe are very happy about this."

The trio hugged each other. Then Tia grabbed Mistletoe and snuggled him in her arms.

Ian hugged his new fiancée. "That day I rescued you, Bri, He rescued me. He's the great physician and I promise to honor Him with our love, always and forever."

"Always and forever," she repeated, and leaned in to collect the kiss and his promise of a lifetime.

He picked Tia into his arms, delighted when Tia squeezed his neck with the same heartfelt expression as Bri.

Ian hugged his daughter tight and also his wife-to-be.

Closed his eyes and thanked God for recovering his lost faith and for rescuing his future family.

* * * * *

If you enjoyed this story by Cheryl Wyatt,
be sure to look for the third book in the
EAGLE POINT EMERGENCY *series,*
coming soon from Love Inspired Books!

Dear Reader,

I am so thankful that you have taken time to read my book. Your support and encouragement means so much. I hope you have a community around you as caring as the friends in fictional Eagle Point. When I'm not writing, I am usually praying. If you need prayer for anything, please don't hesitate to send a request to my "Prayer Box," better known as my Inbox: cheryl@cherylwyatt.com.

I love connecting with readers and mentoring aspiring authors. Visit my website at www.cherylwyatt.com to sign up for my quarterly newsletter for new-release news, giveaways and other fun stuff. I provide free writing prompts to aspiring authors and book recommendations for readers on my blog. Connect with me on Facebook: www.facebook.com/CherylWyattAuthor, where I give away frequent e-readers, exclusive opportunities to name characters and settings in my books, and more!

Cheryl Wyatt

Questions for Discussion

1. Fear and past pain caused Ian to brood around Bri. In what ways do you think Ian could have coped that would have been more healthy for everyone involved?

2. Have you had someone in your life whose personality was altered by physical pain or emotional anguish? How did you cope? Was that person ever you? How did you move past it?

3. Tia hadn't seen her dad since she was two years old. Could you understand her reticence to get close to him?

4. Just when Bri thought things couldn't get worse, she took a tumble off a ladder and broke her arm. Do you think God forces us into situations where we have to depend on others at times?

5. Why do you think we have such a tough time receiving help? Could you understand why Bri did? At what point did she turn around, and what do you think made the difference?

6. What do you think it was about Bri that caused Tia to grow so close to her quickly?

7. In what ways do you think Bri's abandonment by her own father helped Tia to relate to her? Have you had trauma in your life that enabled you to help others through trauma later? Please discuss.

8. At what point in the story do you feel Ian should have stopped covering for Ava? Do you think this ultimately helped Tia, or put off her acceptance longer than necessary? How would you have handled the situation if you were Ian?

9. What do you think were the deeper reasons for Tia's acting out? What do you think made the most difference in getting through to Tia?

10. What was your favorite scene and why?

11. Which secondary character(s) would you like to see have their own story?

12. Could you understand Ian's rift with God? How do you cope with disappointment in your own life, with regard to your faith walk?

LARGER-PRINT BOOKS!

GET 2 FREE LARGER-PRINT NOVELS PLUS 2 FREE MYSTERY GIFTS

Love Inspired

Larger-print novels are now available...

Love Inspired® SUSPENSE

RIVETING INSPIRATIONAL ROMANCE

Watch for our series of edge-
of-your-seat suspense novels.
These contemporary tales
of intrigue and romance
feature Christian characters
facing challenges to their faith...
and their lives!

AVAILABLE IN REGULAR
& LARGER-PRINT FORMATS

For exciting stories that reflect traditional values,
visit:
www.ReaderService.com

LISUSDIR11B

Reader Service.com

Manage your account online!

- Review your order history
- Manage your payments
- Update your address

> ## We've designed the Reader Service website just for you.

Enjoy all the features!

- Reader excerpts from any series
- Respond to mailings and special monthly offers
- Discover new series available to you
- Browse the Bonus Bucks catalogue
- Share your feedback

Visit us at:

ReaderService.com